Rimini Revisited

Diana Bettinson

Copyright © 2019 Diana Bettinson

All rights reserved.

ISBN:9781916162402

This little story is dedicated to my wonderful family who put up with me all the time.

ACKNOWLEDGMENTS

Thank you for all your help and encouragement my proofreader and husband John, Claire Walker who also does proof reading and encouragement. Suzan Collins who read it through and helped with lots of mistakes.

A "cheer up" holiday after her divorce, what could possibly go wrong? Fran and her friend Jess set off to Rimini, thinking it would be nice to relive some of the memories of her last visit as a teenager. The time when love blossomed. He wouldn't still be there would he? Anyway, he would be married by now with lots of children. Wouldn't he?

After all the promised letters swearing undying love had never arrived, had they? He had forgotten all about her, hadn't he?

Was it a mistake? Should she ever have tried to revisit her past?

CHAPTER 1

FRAN

'Are you all packed then Fran?' Jess demanded on the phone. 'I know what you're like. I'll bet you were sitting there daydreaming.'

Indeed, the phone call had interrupted my thoughts while I was supposed to be packing for our holiday. I spend a lot of time thinking, maybe I over think things. My dear friend Jess and I were going for a quick break to Rimini. We could've gone anywhere within reason, and this time it was my choice. Next holiday it'll be Jess' turn to choose.

Of course, that's where I met Pieta, the boy I fell in love with, and his friend Paulo. I was attracted to Pieta as soon as I saw him. Working as a waiter in the café my parents and I went to for our morning coffee. Big soulful brown eyes framed with long black lashes, ones that any supermodel would die for, and black wavy silky hair. Finely chiselled features and even at the age of eighteen he had a fit and muscled body. He was always dressed in crisp white shirt, black trousers for work and the shiniest black shoes, even on the hottest days. He must have spent hours polishing those shoes. He seemed to be attracted to me, in his shy serious way, but then it's a bit of a cliché for English girls to fall in love with Italian waiters. I was also eighteen and on holiday with my parents. In fact, it was the last holiday they had together.

The cracks in their marriage were showing and growing daily. It worried me at the time, and I was sad that I could see what was coming even before they did. Their divorce followed soon after that holiday.

But Pieta? Well he left an indelible mark on my memory. Just a holiday fling, I did give him my address, but I never heard from him again. I was so disappointed because although I knew of the reputation of the likes of Pieta and his friend Paulo, he did swear undying love. 'My bella regazza, how can I let you out of my life? I must be able to touch your soul, even from afar.'

Such flowery words had indeed touched the heart and soul of this silly, just out of school, girl. Fool that I was I believed him. Was I so naive at that age? I shouldn't have expected anything else really, but this felt different and I came to believe that he really did love me. So, coming home from that fateful holiday I got on with life, although I still waited for the promised letters and cried often for the lost love I left in Italy. It was quite soon after coming home that I met Ray, on a girly night out in town. He was a student in computer something or other. I still hankered after Pieta but realised that was an impossible situation. I had to face reality, that Italian boy was never going to be part of my life. Ray and I got on well, made each other laugh and cry. I thought I'd found love again. We got married, even before he finished his studies. I made myself put the 'Two Ps' as Dad called them, Pieta and Paulo to the back of my mind and accept the normality of daily life.

Guiltily I told Jess that I was nearly done. And pulled myself even further out of my reverie.

'Well get on with it, woman. The taxi will he here in about ten minutes, then we'll be round for you. You've got about half an hour to get sorted. And don't forget to put those nice dresses in that we bought last week.'

'Yes mam,' I said laughing at her bossiness. Putting the phone down I went to get the dresses she was talking about. Not really my style, a bit too revealing for me, but I supposed they'd look alright once I had a tan. Jess had insisted that we go shopping for new clothes for me as I only had either smart work clothes or very casual wear. None of which fitted me properly now anyway and many of them were taking casual to a new low level. Most of my clothes should be thrown out because they were just about fit to be used as dusters.

I'd only very recently divorced and was still feeling a bit delicate. It's probably a silly time to be going away because I've had a new studio built and it's nearly finished. The one good thing Ray did for me was to make me concentrate on my own company and business, my graphics workspace is now in the garden where his beloved summer house used to be. I always hated that summer house, glad to get rid of it.

Oh blast, that's Jess with the taxi and I am clearly not ready. Quickly stuffing the rest of my clothes in the case and making sure I had the money and my passport I went down to let her in. She looked resplendent as usual. In a black top and her pristine white jeans. I had to admire her; I had a pair of white jeans once, but they never left the house. I would mess them up before I ever got out of the door.
I just had my old but comfortable jeans on and a pink tee shirt.

'Taxi for Mrs. Middleton, or should that be Ms. Middleton?'
Hoping I'd not forgotten anything vital; I loaded my case and bag in the boot and got in the cab.

'We're all going on a summer holiday,' Jess sang as the cab pulled away. 'Well a late spring one anyway.'

'Did I lock the door?' I asked in terror.

'Yeah, I saw you, anyway, your Mum'll be round shortly to check on everything for you. Won't she?'

'Yes, and have a good rummage around while she's there,' I answered.

'Anyway, never mind all that now, let's just enjoy this holiday. It'll do you good and may even cheer you up a bit. Do you think that Italian lad you fell in love with will still be there?'

'Ha! I hardly think so, he's probably married with a dozen kids, fat around the middle and bald as a coot by now. Where does that saying come from anyway? Coot's aren't bald.'

'Well, bald can mean white stripes as well. Coots definitely have them.'

'Oh, didn't know that. Mine of information, aren't you?'

'I have my uses,' she smiled. 'Anyway, we can have a nice boozy night in the hotel before we go to Stanstead tomorrow.'

'Oh God, I don't want to be drinking much if I'm flying tomorrow, I've flown with a hangover before and it's not nice, believe me.'

'Yes, I remember that, drinking tequila shots, probably not the best way to spend the last day of a holiday. Alright white wine spritzer it is for you, light weight. Do you know? Even so early in the season we should be in for some lovely weather, I've looked it up and it's about twenty-five degrees and sunny there. Roll on the sunshine.'

Glancing out I emphasised with her feeling there, looking at the grey cloudy sky above us and the drizzle laying its own fine mist on the window.

'Brilliant and seeing as it's just before the bank holiday and we got those flights really cheap. "£97.00," return, did you say? Can't beat that. I only hope the pictures of the hotel were real and not just some artist's impressions. Don't want to be in the middle of a building site.'

'Huh, just put your bikini on and give the builders something to look at.' Jess laughed. The taxi driver was enjoying our conversation as well.

'Those builders'll never finish the hotel if the two of you parade in front of them,' he said. We all had a good giggle. I really was beginning to look forward to this break, Jess will never let me stay sad for long, she's brilliant at cheering me up.

On reaching the airport hotel we unloaded our bags with the help of our friendly taxi driver, and went to book in. We'd decided on one night here which is a bit of a luxury really as we only live about twenty miles away from the airport. But it's the only holiday I'm having this year. Jess is also divorced, and we are "Ladies that do." Although my divorce has only been final for a few weeks. Jess has been in this position for nearly three years. She was just as devastated as me when it happened to her, I spent many an hour sitting with her while she cried, ranted, and raved. And cried some more. But she's now my support and shoulder to cry on. Especially as Ray has already re-married.

'We can get to the airport nice and early tomorrow, if you've forgotten anything, we can buy it in the duty free,' Jess was saying butting into my reverie again.

'What? Oh yes of course,' I muttered.

'Come on woman, get with the program. We have some serious holidaying to do. No sad stuff for at least a week. Then? Yeah okay, it's back to the grindstone for us both to save for the next one.'

'You're right. Holiday time it is, although I've never had to grind my own flour.' I said forcing a smile on my still rather sad face.

'Oh, you've been looking up the meanings of popular sayings, have you?'

'Well I haven't got your amazing memory, thank goodness for the internet,' I said smiling properly this time. I wondered if it's true what they say about smiling, the more it of you do the happier you feel.

So, having spent a pleasant evening in the hotel we were nice and early at the airport the next day. I said to Jess, 'We mustn't get carried away shopping and miss the call to the gate,' as she headed into a changing room.

'Don't worry I've got my eye on the departure board all the time,' she assured me.

Six new bikinis and a few nice tee shirts between us we headed to the gate to get on the plane. The only trouble with cheap seats is that we can't be promised to sit together. Jess was three rows ahead of me. I'd have liked her with me to keep chatting, then I wouldn't have time to think about the last time I went on a plane, with Ray. But the lovely Italian lady beside me had all of two and a half hours to tell me her life story, so I didn't have time to think any sad thoughts. She told me that her son Pieta, had just completed a new hotel project and it had only been open for a few weeks. She lived in England with her sister who had married an English man. It made sense she said to be together.

'As we are both widowed, we decided to set up home together. Why my sister wanted to remain in such a cold place is beyond me. But we're not lonely at least, and I can visit my family often.'

'She didn't want to come with you then. Your sister?'

'She comes sometimes but most of her family are in England so she can drive to see them.'

This nice lady hoped that her son was going to meet her

at the airport, and she was going to visit his new hotel for a few days before she went to stay with her daughter. And Pieta? There must be thousands of Pieta's in Italy, so it would be totally unreasonable to think it was the same one. But my stomach did a flip, anyway. Her son had been a hard worker but to her great sorrow he had never married.

'I want more grand children before I am too old to enjoy them.'

'But Pieta, he never got married?'

'With three jobs and saving all his money, I don't think he had the time,' she told me.

'Why did he work so hard?'

'This hotel was his big dream and always the plan, he always said he would be rich and since he used to spend his summers working in Rimini as a young boy, he has always wanted to have his own place there. Right on the Rimini sea front.'

'Well done him,' I said. Summer in Rimini? I thought it must be a coincidence that this ladies' son was called Pieta and he worked in Rimini in the summer.

'He needs a wife and I want more grandchildren to bring me joy in my old age.'

'How many do you have now?'

'Just the five, and I want more. I love them all so much.'

'Gosh, you don't look old enough to have grandchildren.'

'Thank you, my dear. That's very kind of you. I do like to look after myself.'

Soon it was landing time and we stood to get off the plane. Opening the overhead locker, I helped her get her bags down. Then made sure I had gathered all mine, the new tee shirts and bikinis, mustn't leave those behind. As we stepped down from the plane, I noticed Jess wasn't carrying any bags. A man standing beside her had them all. Shaking my head in amusement I thought, she soon found a slave. At passport control he handed her the shopping and went on his merry way. We got through baggage claim uneventfully and walked purposefully out of the airport into the bright Italian sunshine. Oh, it was so nice to feel the warmth and see the sun. The lady I was sitting next to also came out at the same time to be greeted by her son, I assumed. Phew! I thought, not my Pieta then, I could let my racing heart calm down. There was a lady and two children with him, who all greeted my fellow passenger with many kisses and hugs and loud Italian salutations. She was happy to see the family that had come to welcome her home. I heard the word 'Pieta' but of course as they were speaking in very fast Italian, I couldn't make out anything else they said. She glanced over and looked sad.

'I wish you a lovely holiday, my dear. As usual Pieta couldn't come to meet me. He is always so busy.'

'Well I hope you see him soon and can drag him away from work. Have a lovely stay with your family,' my thoughts racing again, but I told myself not to be so silly, it couldn't be him. My Pieta.
Already her attention was pulled back to her family. That cheered me up, seeing such joy.

Chapter 2

Fran

Jess and I went off to find a taxi to take us to the hotel and settled down to enjoy the ride. Jess asked me how the flight was and proceeded to tell me all about the man she had been talking to. An English businessman who was here to try to source some fine Italian wine for his shops in England.

'He nearly didn't make the flight, stuck in a huge traffic jam apparently. So good job we stayed at the hotel last night or we may've been stuck in it as well.'

'I was being regaled with the complete life story of a nice Italian lady, coming to see her son Pieta,' I said quietly.

'Really? Still Italy must be full of Pietas,' she said. 'Well I'm glad I wasn't next to her; I wouldn't have fancied being talked at all the way through the flight.'

My friend is a talker, not a listener. So, I expect she would have had a torrid time trying to get a word in sideways with my elegant Italian companion. I, on the other hand, have difficulty making small talk. I enjoyed not having to think of something interesting to say.

When we arrived at our holiday accommodation, we were both very impressed by The Bacchus hotel. Far from being a building site it was beautifully finished and all bright, shiny and new looking. We were given the key cards to our room and made our way up in the spacious lift. The cases were already there. Wow! What service.

'Phew, this is five-star luxury. We didn't need to bring those plug adapters, look there are English plug points and American ones. And just look at the bathroom, we'll have to run around in that shower just to get wet,' I enthused at the sight of our room. 'And two double beds so no being cramped up in little single ones.'

'Just look at all this wardrobe space as well,' she answered, flinging all the doors open.

'Right, get into something summery and let's go and see where we can have a cool drink. We can unpack later,' Jess ordered me as she slung her case on her bed and opening it, she fished out a strappy summer dress and gave me a knowing look. So, I followed suit and we went down to find a nice cool refreshing drink. We could have stayed in the hotel on the terrace but after sitting for so long on the plane I fancied a bit of a walk. We didn't walk very far though.

Just outside the hotel and across the road on the beach we spied a bar, which we assumed, belonged to the hotel. Jess said it would be a nice stop off and take in the surroundings. As we approached, we saw that it did in fact belong to the hotel.

'A good place to do some talent spotting.' Jess was always on the lookout for the next boyfriend.

'Man hunting? I'm not up for that, but I could do with a cold drink. And just look at that glorious beach.'

We found a place to sit and ordered white wine, nice and cold. Staring out towards the beach which was as beautiful as the brochure had said, deep blue sea with small waves lapping onto the lovely golden sand. There were plenty of families dotted around and I was happy just to watch the children playing in the surf. What a relaxing way to start a holiday. It's a good job I'd put on some heavy-duty high factor protection as my lily-white legs would need plenty of acclimatization before I dared to risk the sun full on them, I don't get them out very often. After a couple of glasses of delicious cool wine, we headed back to the hotel room to unpack and get ready for the evening meal.

The beds had been turned down for us and a sweetie had been placed on each pillow. Jess went for a shower first while I flicked through the leaflets to see where we should visit. I knew I'd have a hard time getting her off the sunbeds either on the beach or round the pool. Jess was never one to sit still for long, but it wasn't a holiday for her unless she got plenty of sunbathing time. However, with a whole week to fill I didn't think I could just sit around all day every day. I ticked a couple excursions for us to try from the hotel information pack. I left these for Jess to peruse while I went next into the shower. What lovely soft water. It took ages for me the rinse the shampoo out of my hair. That spacious shower was real luxury. Coming back through I plugged in my travel hairdryer. But Jess opened a draw to show me that here was one already in there for us to use. She had hung up all our dresses and had gone to the trouble of picking one for me to wear tonight. Of course, one of the ones we'd bought together, but I decided I needed a bit of colour before I could wear it, so swapped it for a slightly less revealing one. Ignoring the resigned look on her face.

'Ha! I knew you'd chicken out of wearing that one. But rest assured my lady, you will be wearing both of those dresses before the week is out.'

'Not together, I hope.'

'Oh, was that a joke? First, I've heard from you for months. Good, that's more like it.'

'Better take a wrap with us. It may get chilly later in the evening,' I said.

'Always the practical one,' Jess said as she picked up a pashmina, the colour of which blended perfectly with the dress she was wearing. We went down in the lift to the dining room, where we were shown to a table with a view of the whole restaurant.

'Oh dear, I am going to go home a couple of sizes bigger if we eat here every night,' I said looking at the menu. Still a bit worried about putting on that weight again.

'It's what holidays are for,' she answered.

My weight had always fluctuated. I remember moaning about it to Mum when I was younger.

'That Jess, never still, even when she is just sitting, she jiggles about. Lots of nervous energy. And she's skinny, not slim. Anyway, boys like a few curves.'

'I don't care what boys like, I just wish I was slim like Jess.'

'Oh, and look like a flat chested youth? Don't be silly, you're nice and round.'

'I'm fat. '

I had kept my weight stable for so many years. Until the divorce. And the comfort eating. When I blossomed, but not for the right reasons.

Jess was chatting and hadn't realised I had gone into another reverie.

Then I saw him. Pieta, my Pieta. He looked far from being fat and married with a dozen kids, and he had just as much hair as he did in my memories. He escorted the lady from the plane into the dining room. My heart almost stopped, and my mouth went dry. I just wished I could curl up in a corner and disappear. I ducked my head, but she saw us and stopped by for a chat while he organised tables for the family.

'Oh, my dear, let me introduce my son Pieta,' she turned and called him over. 'I was telling this nice young lady all about you and your hotel,' she said to Pieta. 'Here we have Guilia my daughter and her husband Ricardo and their children Maurizio and

Marianne. This is the young lady who kept me company on the flight.'

I only had eyes for Pieta and as he looked deep into my soul with those dark brown eyes he simply said.

'Hello Fran.'

Chapter 3

Pieta.

I could just about get the words out. 'Hello Fran'. There was so much I wanted to say but, as I had been hiding my emotions for so long that I realised it sounded cold and distant. The words came out as a command, rather than a greeting. I never thought I'd see her again. My heart was bouncing around in my chest and my speech wouldn't come out right.

There she was, the girl I fell in love with all those years ago. She still with her long straight silky blond hair, slightly darker but as beautiful as ever. And those bright eyes were just as sparkly and compelling. Still finding it hard to talk I just wanted to hold her and hug her. But I managed to croak a hello. She looked as if she was having trouble talking as well. As I looked at her, I could see embarrassment and confusion. Why was she here and where's her husband? She was wearing a ring so there must be one, and probably children, how many? I feel so embarrassed and ashamed now thinking of all those letters I wrote to her which she never replied too.

We were eighteen and she was staying in Rimini with her parents and I noticed she was different straight away. Not brash and blousy, but quiet and intense. Although we had fun while she was here, seeing her now was sending my heart into tumult. It rocked my neatly ordered, wrapped up world and rendered my body in a spasm of paralysis. I had put that all away at the back of my mind and got on with my plan to be rich. Mamma was calling me to sort out the table arrangements. I really wanted to speak more with this lovely lady. I stood, looking at the face of my memories, unable to move or speak. I had many questions to ask her but that would have to wait. Mamma's imperious voice reached into my mind at last and with a curt nod to Fran and her friend I made my way to our family table. Mamma asked me if I knew the lady she had been chatting to on the plane and as I looked over at Fran she knew.

'That's her isn't it? The one who broke your heart all those years ago. But My son, she is married, I've seen her ring. But what does she want to come back here for? She should leave you alone and go home.'

'She had every right to come on holiday Mamma. She wouldn't know this is my hotel. How could she?'

'No, indeed, how could she as she didn't even have the curtesy to answer your letters. How she must have laughed at the poor Italian boy that she pretended to love. Just went home and got married. Ha!'

Fran had been here with her parents. Paulo had seen her first and began to flirt with her unmercifully. It's all he could think of in those days.

'Watch me,' he said. 'I will steal her away from right under her parents' noses.' So, I watched and the more he flirted the more amused I saw Fran become. She would giggle, but as Paulo walked away each time, she cast an amused glance at her father. I'm afraid to say it, but I had a sneaky satisfaction when I realised, they were in fact laughing at Paulo's antics. I was so much quieter in those days, really quite shy. She liked that, and we were attracted to each other. Paulo, to do him justice, shrugged and said,

'You win this one, my friend.' He soon found another English beauty to give his undivided attention to. However, I fell in love with this beautiful young lady and the more time we could spend together during that holiday the more I felt for her. Can you do that in two weeks? Apparently, you can as I did. I begged her to give me her address in England so that I could continue the contact by letter. I could see she was sceptical and expected me to be like all the other waiters. Those who only wanted to flirt with someone for the duration of the holiday then on to the next one. But I thought I had convinced her that my heart was true.

'How will I continue to live here knowing you're so far away and have taken my heart with you to England?'

'Oh, Pieta, I will, I'll come back to Italy to be with you. I've fallen in love with this place and with you. I want to be with you forever.'

We spent may happy hours talking, sharing dreams of our futures. I told her I was going to be rich and own at least one hotel maybe a whole chain of them. She smiled at my enthusiasm and told me she was heading for art school. She was already working part time in a graphic design studio. She showed me some of her pictures and paintings. I asked if I could have one. The very next day she presented me with a water colour painting of the sea front and coast. It is a marvellous painting and I still have it hanging in my office. She signed it 'To Pieta with all my love Fran.' I remember sitting with her while she painted or sketched. Happy to just be in her company. So talented and so beautiful, her hair so long and straight, and those green eyes that sparked turquoise in some lights and turned bluer when she was quiet. I remembered some of our talks and how we made each other laugh.

'Fran, it is short for some other name?'

'Yes,' she giggled. 'Short for Frances.'

'After Saint Francis, of Assisi?'

'Well, not quite, short for Francis, with an "I" yes but I

was named after my Dad, who I consider a saint.'

'But he is Frank?'

'Uh-hu, Frank is the man's way of shortening Francis. As in Frank Sinatra. But the girl's way is spelled with an "e". So, we have both. And you are named after Saint Peter? Keeper of the gates?

'Yes, and I am of course a saint.'

Oh. the memories brought back to reality by the sharp slap on my hand from Mamma. Back to the time and place and to try to concentrate on my family.

Chapter 4
Fran

I could just about squeak 'Hello Pieta.' He just stood there looking as if he had more to say. I was totally tongue tied by that time but could feel my heart beating out a tattoo in my chest. His mother called him and with a curt nod of his head he went over to where they were all sitting, at a large table in the middle of the restaurant. Obviously' there were more of them to come, and I expected to see another woman arrive with his children. But the next members of the party were another husband and wife with three more children. And that filled the table.

Jess finally unlocked her drooping jaw. I'd never know her to be so quiet.

'Not at all chubby around the middle then, of course he still could have the dozen kids at home,' she joked. I found it hard to talk and just wanted to get away. So much for getting fat I could hardly eat any of the delicious food that was put in front of us.

I realised that I did in fact know one member of the second family to arrive. It was none other than Paulo. So, the two Ps were still friends then. He greeted the older lady with such affection that I assumed he must be the husband of the other sister.

Finally, when Jess decided she had eaten enough we were able to get away. As we left the restaurant, I felt Pieta's eyes following me out. Jess wanted to go to the bar and have another glass of wine so reluctantly I followed her.

'You're very quiet? It's a bit of a coincidence that we ended up in his hotel though isn't it?' Jess said not realising how much I'd been affected by seeing Pieta again. I felt all the longing and desire that I'd felt all those years ago.

'I need to get away,' I said.

'Okay we'll have an early night.' She went to the bar and asked for two glasses of white wine to take up with us.

'No, I need to really get away. I'm going home. We should never have come here,' I told her as we walked to the lift.

'What? Don't be silly. We'd never get a flight.'
Back up in our room I threw myself across the bed and sobbed. I now knew that I had really been in love with this man and was reliving my broken heart. He'd let me down and now the emotions cursing around in my head were nothing short of torture. He'd sworn undying love but had not thought a thing about me as soon as I left Italy. He had probably just gone on to the next silly girl, to get off a plane. The promised letters didn't arrive. I thought I'd be alright if I did get to see him again after all this time. I really thought I would be able to look at him and smile at the memories. But the surge of love for this man hit me like a brick wall and knocked me sideways.

Oh yes, he'd aged and didn't look like the eighteen-year-old waiter I fell for, but he was definitely not the fat contented father of twelve I had envisaged. He was Pieta. My Pieta.

'Perhaps I didn't love Ray enough? Maybe that's why he left? Did I always love Pieta and marry Ray on the rebound? Did I give Ray enough? Or was I still holding my heart back from him?'
All this came tumbling out between my sobs. Jess just stroked my shoulder while sitting on my bed.

'Of course, you loved Ray enough, you gave him

everything you could. He took all you had to give and tossed it away, it wasn't your fault that he couldn't see what he had,' she said soothingly.

The whole episode had been very upsetting right from the time Ray had come home to find me crying. I'd found all the bank statements he'd been trying to hide from me. The ones that showed his hotel expenses. Talk of clichés. I mean you see it all the time in films and read it in books, but it didn't feel much like a cliché when it happened to me. Ray admitted that he'd been having an affair, that the other woman was also expecting his baby. He packed his bags then and there and left me, for this much younger model.

Our marriage, it would seem, was over. Twelve years of working and keeping a home together for us both while he studied and then built his business. Twelve years of waiting to have a family, supporting him in his education and early years of the company. Now at the age of thirty-three I was thrown aside. To add insult to injury he also had the child with that other woman. He'd asked me to wait and I had done just that. I was not too old even now to have children, but that choice has been taken away from me. And now here's Pieta. Life can throw some bloody awful curveballs sometimes.

At last the sobs were beginning to subside but, I cried myself to sleep and when I woke the next day, I looked at my red rimmed, puffy eyes and thought, well that'll put him off if nothing does. How am I supposed to face anyone with a face like this?

'Ready for breakfast?' Jess asked, always ready to eat.

'I'm not coming down.'

'Oh yes you are, you hardly ate any of your dinner last night and you'll be fainting on me soon. I'll sit here and

wait while you have a shower and get prettied up.'
Jess settled down with a magazine on the balcony and I knew she meant what she said.

'Can't we just have breakfast up here on the balcony?' I asked. 'It'll give me a bit more time to prepare myself.'

'Look, if you really want to go home, we need to go to reception to organise some flights. Which means you must leave this room. The sooner you face up to what is frightening you the better,' she said reasonably.

'We don't really have to go home; I was in shock last night. I feel better now. Maybe I've cried it all out.'

'Okay, that's good, but you're not spending the next week in this room. Get washed, and come down to breakfast, I'm starving. You can't let him get to you. He was a holiday fling, nothing more. There's no need to be embarrassed.'

Oh, Jess, how little you know. Embarrassment wasn't my primary emotion right now.

'That doesn't make me feel any better, knowing I was just a silly kid who fell for the charms of a Lothario.'

'Well, not quite one of them, but you can't let him spoil all the hard work you've done since the divorce. You've come so far and there's a world of love out there just waiting for you to realise it.'

I was feeling somewhat fragile as we went down to the breakfast terrace. At least I wouldn't look too out of place wearing my ultra-big sun shades, to cover up the puffy eyes, while sitting in the early morning sunshine. I'd come out ready for poolside. I had a bikini on under my pale blue shift dress. Jess had on a pink flowery dress and a large sunhat, looking for all the world like a celebrity trying to be incognito.

All through breakfast I was on edge looking for Pieta. He'd be around, I was sure. He owned the hotel. Even with family visiting he would have to keep an eye on how things were running. I did manage to eat something, a small piece of toast and had several cups of coffee. Jess had been looking at the excursions I'd ticked and noted that the meeting with the rep was at ten o'clock. There was no hurry to leave.

'The rep comes here to the terrace so we can have some more coffee while we wait,' Jess said.

We carried on sitting there and I kept a look out for Pieta. What would I do if, and when, I saw him? I didn't know but as scared as I was, I really wanted to see him, talk to him. I was a nervous wreck by the time the rep appeared. Jess and I booked two trips out, paid for them and then wandered down to the pool area where we stood looking for some sun beds and a sunshade. It seemed that there were some beds but only a few where free and they were all separate, with no shade. People seemed to get up early around here.

Jess said. 'Well, only one thing for it we need to pinch a couple of beds and find a brolly somewhere.'

Chapter 5

Pieta

Standing on the breakfast terrace overlooking the pool area I saw Fran and her friend looking for chairs. I picked up the bar phone and put a call through to Mario down by the pool.

'Can you get some chairs an umbrella and table for the two English Ladies please Mario?' I wanted to go down and arrange it myself, so I could be a bit closer to the girl I loved all those years ago, but I knew Mamma was about to come down and wouldn't approve of my talking to her, in fact it would give her another chance to remonstrate with me. At least I had the satisfaction of making Fran comfortable.

But Mamma? Once, Mamma discovered just who this lady was that she'd been talking to on the plane she came over all protective. She decided she didn't like the, English Woman, as she put it and I knew that she wouldn't let me near her to be hurt again. I wondered if I'd be able to get out of the planned visit to Guilia's house, but I doubt that somehow. Mamma would have a fit, if I dared suggest it. How I would have loved to go down and talk to her, Fran. I found myself taking glances at her all last evening and I couldn't tell you anything of the conversation that was going around the table. Paulo recognised her as well.

'She is still alive then, my friend,' he said to me
'And still very beautiful,' I answered.
'Ah, so you do have some romance in that brain of yours, not just the obsessive business builder. But yes, I agree, she is still beautiful. Your English run away.'
'She didn't run away Paulo, she went home.'

'And forgot all about you, don't let that little snippet slip your mind.'

'Yes, and by the looks of her hand she married as well.' I said sadly.

Standing here today, on this balcony longing to touch and hold the woman of my dreams, the one who spoiled me for any other. But I stood here just watching. Watching and longing.

Chapter 6

Fran

Suddenly there was a bit of a commotion as two waiters cleared a space and pulled over two sun loungers. They also brought a brolly and a table out from a shed near the pool. These were set up for us and we were given two towels each from the pool side store. Jess was, I could tell, most impressed at the service, although she graciously accepted it as her due. It caused a bit of chatter amongst the other hotel guests as well. I wondered if they thought Jess was somebody they should recognise.

I looked around straight into the soulful eyes of Pieta who was standing on the breakfast terrace watching the proceedings. I smiled almost involuntarily, and he nodded back, but no smile. Oh dear. This is going to be harder than I thought. He really did only think of me as another poor little naïve English girl who let herself fall in love with a handsome Italian waiter. How he must be laughing now. Him and Paulo.

'Did you bring your sunscreen down with you? And your book?' Jess asked after she had ordered two ice cold colas for us to drink.

'Yes, I have both here and your sunscreen as well. You don't want to go getting burnt. Even though you've already got a good tan, from the sun beds,' I warned her.

'Alright mummy. Give it here and I'll slap some on.' Throughout the day Jess amused herself by giving the waiters a score from one to ten for looks, also the lifeguards and some of the holiday guests. I kept telling her to shush in case one of them heard her, but undaunted she carried on with her game. I could see the funny side of it and found it really quite amusing. I must admit I did have a bit of a giggle when, as we were packing up our things to go back to our room after a day baking in the sunshine, one of the said waiters came over ask asked what his score was. Poor Jess coloured up to a very bright red and that wasn't due to the sun.

'Ten out of ten, of course,' she said regaining her composure amazingly quickly. He went off with a smile as well. 'Well at least I cheered up someone today,' she muttered as we made our way in, and we both exploded into a full giggling fit as soon as we reached our room. She really knows how to brighten my day.

Later that evening as we were seated in the dining room, I looked forward to some fantastic Italian food. Hungry, as I hadn't eaten much the night before. I asked for a chicken dish, of course accompanied by the superb wine. I saw Pieta's mother across the room, but she studiously ignored me. In fact, I would go so far as to say that she gave me the cold shoulder. I wondered what I'd done to cause this turn around. She'd been so friendly and welcoming but now was decidedly unfriendly. Pieta didn't join her this evening but Guilia and the children were with her. He probably has work to do, I thought. Although dreading it I really wanted to see him. I felt a wave of disappointment wash over me as Jess and I ate our delicious meal. But as Jess said I couldn't allow them to spoil this holiday. Then on, into the bar for another glass of the superb house wine. Or two. We were joined by another English couple who we discovered were on their honeymoon.

'What do you think of the Hotel?' Jess asked Leigh.

'Oh, it's lovely isn't it. Of course, we have the honeymoon suite. It's gorgeous, we have a huge balcony with a hot tub. And such a big bed. I may lose him, if I'm not careful.'

'No chance of that.' Mike said, 'I'm not letting you out of my sight. Anyway, we won't be using all of it, will we?' He added with a raise of the eyebrows. Leigh giggled and blushed. They stayed and chatted for just one drink and then wandered hand in hand off to their room

'Aw, loves young dream. Shall we take one up with us?' Jess asked as she finished her glass. 'We can sit on the balcony and watch the late Italian world go by.'
I quickly slurped the rest of my drink down and we asked at the bar for some to take to our room.

Jess hesitated slightly on her way to the bar but squared her shoulders and walked purposefully to order our drinks. Then I saw why.

'You would like if I brought this up to your bedroom?' asked the, "ten out of ten waiter", from the pool side with a knowing smile and a wink.
I quickly cut in before Jess could say anything else to embarrass us.

'No, thank you, we'll just carry them.' Elbowing her in the ribs and trying not to snigger. Quite how Jess got hers up there without spilling it I don't know; she was giggling so much.

'Think I may have made a conquest there. Not the Roman conquest but at least a Rimini one.'
Oh dear, Jess has had too much to drink, I thought. We settled on the balcony which overlooked the beach and marvelled at the gorgeous view of the dark sea gently lapping on the shore. Then I saw him, Pieta, he left the hotel and walked across the road to where a large car was parked. He got int it and reversed out of the parking space and as he drove past the hotel he looked up and straight into my eyes. He nodded in my direction, still not smiling, and drove away. Jess hadn't

noticed as she was still playing her game with the men walking along the street.

'Definitely a ten there,' she stated. I was pulled away from my thoughts to look and saw a very red-faced man who I thought must be English.

'Ten for looks? Really?'

'No, ten for not putting enough sun cream on,' she laughed. 'Poor chap, that looks really sore. Oh gosh, I've just remembered we booked one of those trips out, tomorrow didn't we?' she continued. 'What time do we need to get up for that?'
Picking up the wallet with our tickets and times in I scanned the itinerary. 'Bus picks us up from the front of the hotel at nine. So early breakfast for us.'

'Shall I set the alarm on my phone?' I asked as we clambered into our spacious beds.

'Yeah, better,' she said already dozing off. 'Don't want to be late, do we?'
I couldn't help but feel relieved that I wouldn't have to spend the whole day on the lookout for Pieta, but contrarily I was disappointed that we had to go out as well. In case I missed seeing him. I just wished my heart would make up its mind one way or the other. Although I was glad that we could be out of Mrs. Bianchi's way. She was quite intimidating with her attitude towards me after that first night. I didn't want to give her the opportunity to snub me again.

I spent a restless night, listening to Jess' slightly tipsy snoring. Wine always sent Jess to sleep, but it seemed to have the opposite effect on me tonight. In the morning, still feeling a bit tired we dressed in vest tops and shorts, well denim cut offs for me. Then, went down to breakfast, making sure on our way that the weather would be nice enough for what we were wearing. I checked that we had sunscreen, tickets, and money, we waited outside the front for the bus. The hotel had supplied us with a packed lunch to take with us. We were going on a vineyard tour. It was an all-day excursion and we would be visiting several vineyards in the area.

'I'm sort of looking forward to this. I can have a few hairs of the dog. I'm feeling a bit under the weather today.' She'd drunk far more than I had and was feeling, as she put it, a bit delicate today.

'Well it doesn't show; you look all perky and bright eyed. Where does that one come from anyway.

'What under the weather? It's a maritime phrase, meaning feeling seasick. Especially when it's windy.' Leigh and Mike were standing on the hotel steps as well, waiting for the same bus tour.

'I always wondered where that saying came from,' said Leigh.

'Ah, well you see, Jess knows them all, if you need a saying explained, I can offer my friend.'
Jess swept her big hat off with a flourish and curtsied. 'Ouch,' she said cramming the hat back on and pulling out her designer sunglasses. 'That sun hurts the eyes.' We were all giggling as we filed onto the bus.

By lunch time when the bus pulled into the car park of the third farm Jess was feeling so much better. She recognised the man she had been talking to on the plane who was dressed very smartly. Obviously, this was one of the yards he wanted to do business with. Jess, I noticed, went into full flirt mode. Hmm, she's feeling more herself, I thought. I turned and started to follow the group into the building for the obligatory wine tasting but as I turned, I bumped into someone standing right behind me.

'Pieta?'

'Welcome to my home,' he said. Still no smile. In fact, his voice was cold and unfriendly.

'You live here? You own this as well? Gosh you have done well.'

'Is that a surprise? I always said I would be rich if you remember.'

'Oh yes, I remember. I remember it well. There are a lot of things I remember.' I said feeling tears gather in my eyes. I couldn't help myself, the tears rolled down my cheeks. Why ever was I crying? But all the tension of the last couple of days boiled up in me. I felt him relax and relent. He was still distant as if he really didn't want his past catching up with him. But then he saw I was crying, and he pulled me into his arms where I immediately felt safe and I let the tears flow. The closeness of his body to mine brought with it a rush of emotion the likes of which I haven't felt for many a long day. He held me with tender care and let me cry for a while. Then he took my face in his hands and brushed the tears away with his thumbs, very gently.

'Such emotion Fran, I could almost swear that you are in fact Italian.' Then he let me go and stood back as the others of the party filed into the shop. He turned and walked to his car and drove away, without a backward glance leaving me so very confused. Why would he bother about my tears when he thought so little of me? It was painfully obvious that he didn't want to be anywhere near me. Probably didn't ever expect to see any of the girls he wooed back in the day, ever again.

Jess, having finished flirting and seen her gentleman off in his car to his next port of call came over to me. She was putting a piece of paper into her bag as she came.

'What did he say?'
When I told her, she was just as confused as I was. Why would he come and say hello, if he was just going to walk away? What game is he playing? And why was his mother so cold last night? I couldn't understand what it was that I'd supposedly done.

'Well,' I said giving myself a shake. 'Let's go taste this wine. I feel the need.'
It was delicious and we both knew it was obviously the house wine at the hotel.

'Don't go drinking too much now Jess.' I said trying to lighten the mood. 'You don't want to be blitzed and not want your dinner.' Having said that to her I slurped my second glass of the delicious wine.

'Since when have you known me to be put off my food?'

'True, very true. Nothing stops you from eating.'
After lunch we had one more vineyard to visit and it was back to the various hotels to deposit the other enthusiastic wine testers, many clutching bags that clinked as they made their way down the aisle of the coach. Everyone was a good deal jollier than they had been this morning when they were picked up. We were the last to be dropped off and both had taken a nap on the way back, effects of all that wine? Probably. Maybe we had both drunk too much, but it's a holiday as Jess keeps reminding me.

When we arrived back at the Bacchus, Leigh suggested meeting in the bar before dinner and then sharing a table tonight. I thought their company would take my mind off Pieta for a while, so we arranged to see them at seven.
It was time to go up and get washed and changed for dinner. No time for a dip in the pool today, we went

straight up to make use of the enormous shower and high-speed hairdryer. Feeling much more refreshed after the hot dusty coach trip we went down to dinner.

As we entered the dining room, we encountered Pieta's mother who sniffed and past us with her head held high. She didn't stop to speak. Jess and I looked at each other in total confusion.

'OH, well if that's how she wants to be, then so be it.' I said and spent the rest of the evening studiously ignoring the family, eating far too much. Burying myself in food to cover up my unhappiness. This is what I'd done when Ray upped and left, and I put on all that weight. I told myself that I needed to watch out as those new bikinis wouldn't fit and I'd be bulging out of them. It had taken a while to get my figure back from that bout of over-eating. I didn't want to do it again. At least we had an enjoyable evening hearing all about the joys and disasters of the young couple's wedding. I made sure I was laughing or at least giggling most of the time, just in case Mrs. Bianchi should look our way. I couldn't let her see how miserable I was feeling.

It was becoming a bit of a nightly ritual to have our last glass of wine on the balcony, tonight was no different. Except we had a different bar man serving us one that Jess hadn't given a score to. No winks and suggestions of accompanying us.

'Okay, what's his score?' I asked as we carefully carried our very full glasses to the lift.

'Oh, he's about an eight,' She answered taking a sip.

'Hm, quite a respectable score. I took a hefty gulp of my wine, so I didn't spill any in the lift. And giggling like a couple of schoolgirls we made unsteady progress to our room and settled ourselves comfortably on the balcony.

Again, I saw Pieta go to his car and again he looked directly at me as he drove off. This time though, I thought he looked a bit sad. I wasn't going to let him, and his family spoil this holiday for Jess, or for me. I sat upright and put a virtual steel rod up my back. I thought I'm not going to cower to anybody. If his mother doesn't like me, then I can't help that. I've done nothing wrong. I could still feel his arms around me where he'd held me while I cried today. I would dearly love to be back in those arms.   But let's face it, he never did love me I was just another of those English girls that Italian boys used to try to lure into their beds. I didn't ever get there, but all his protestations of eternal love were just a line he used.

How many girls had he said that to over the years? How many of those had been naïve enough to believe it? Thousands I suspected. He had promised he would write to me and wanted to come to visit. He begged me for my home address which I gave him. It was probably some sort of badge of honour among the waiters. I wondered how many English girls addresses he had collected. He never did write. I never heard from him again. Was he onto the next girl as soon as my plane took off? Probably. How stupid could I have been to believe that I had found the love of my life back then? How am I going to get through the rest of our time here, knowing what I now know? And knowing that he knows it as well? How he and Paulo must be laughing now. Well, all I can do is hold my head high and let them have their laugh. We would be home soon, not soon enough for me. If only I could just get to talk to him.

Chapter 7
Fran

'Beach or pool side?' I asked Jess as we made ourselves ready for our luscious breakfast, although as I was already feeling the tightness around my middle. I decided that I would have to cut down somewhat on the amount of food that was passing my lips. Perhaps just coffee and a little piece of fruit. I also decided that I'd swim lots today either in the sea or in the pool. I didn't want to get flabby. No holiday tummy for me.

'Beach today, I think. I've graded all the pool side waiters,' she joked. 'Time to look further afield.'

'Good, I need to test the water.'

'Is that a metaphoric test? Or are you really going to brave the sea? It'll be cold, it's still very early in the season, the sun won't have had time to warm the water up.'

Had Jess been reading the holiday guide books?

'Good, the colder the better, I need to get some calories burned off. Or I'll have to buy some more clothes just to go home in.'

'Well we've got that other trip into Old Rimini tomorrow, there may be some nice shops for a bit of Itallan "must haves"?'

'Good thinking, if we can afford their fashion clothes, they'll be really expensive. But worth a look,' I was trying to be jolly, even though I didn't feel it.

'Just coffee and orange juice for me please,' I asked the waiter. 'No big breakfast today.'

Jess followed suit and said we can always have some lunch at the beach bar. I always envied Jess, and the amount of food she could pack into that tiny body of hers. I have to admit she's not very often still, always on the move. Of course, she does have her gym membership that she needs to get full value from. I often wonder if she goes there every day to get her daily exercise or to ogle the men that work out there. I can just imagine her moving to another bike or cross trainer to get a closer look at a handsome but unsuspecting fitness freak.

The hotel has its own private beach and we were soon ensconced on sunbeds.

'Slap on the factor and let's get sun baking,' Jess said.

'I think I'll just sit in the shade for a while and then go in for a swim. The day's heating up nicely and I'm sure the water won't be all that chilly, and anyway it's better for burning calories if it's cold.'

'You and your calories, what are they anyway, little bugs that get in the wardrobe and shrink your clothes?'

'Well they don't seem to shrink yours.'

'No, they don't dare,' she laughed.

After about half an hour I thought it was time to dabble my toes and made my way down to the water's edge. The waves that greeted me were indeed quite warm, but I knew as I went in further it'd get colder. 'Well, here goes nothing'. I said to myself and plunged through the waves into the deeper part. It was quite a shock to the system, but I soon got my breath back and swam out a bit. I made sure I kept within the flags that were fluttering on the beach showing the safe places to swim. After about half an hour of swimming back and forth I was beginning to feel the cold of the water and decided I'd burned off enough calories for now. When I got back to our place on the beach and found Jess again, I noticed she was just putting her phone back in her bag.

She looked at me with a rather guilty look on her face.

'Having a nice chat?' I asked.

'Yep,' was all I got back. No long explanation of who she was talking to, no blow by blow, account of the conversation. That in itself was unusual for Jess. Oh well, something very private then I thought. Too private for her best friend? I felt that I was losing out all round. In fact, a little bit lonely.

I dried myself off, slapped on some heavy-duty factor and settled back to read my book. Jess meanwhile was scanning the beach for likely targets to score with her, one to ten, system.

'How will you remember who you have given a ten to or do they get a different score every time you see them?'

'Oh, don't worry, I always remember what mark I've given them, I have this amazing memory for faces, don't forget. Anyway, I have my criteria. Although some of them do look a lot better as they brown off.'

'Oh, right. Does their score change then? Will a five ever become a ten?'

'Oh yes, some of them move up the scale, but I can still remember what their initial score was. Remember my photographic memory.'

But I wasn't totally convinced although I couldn't forget her amazing memory. She never revised for any exams at school, whereas, I'd spend all my spare time trying to learn stuff. Well when I wasn't drawing or painting.

I noticed a man wandering along the beach that I recognised.

'Isn't that the chap you were talking to yesterday?' I asked as he approached.

'Um, yeah,' Jess answered. He was dressed much more casually in shorts and a bright flowery shirt. I surreptitiously looked at him as he walked along. It was obvious that he was looking for someone and when Jess waved to him my suspicions were confirmed. She'd invited him to meet us, or should I say, her today. So that's why she wanted to come to the beach and not stay by the pool. Although this was a private beach that belonged to the hotel is was much more accessible than the hotel pool. And that's why she was so quiet about her phone call.

I was a bit annoyed. Not that she should meet someone but that she felt she had to be so secretive about it. It's as much her holiday as mine and I had no problem if she happened across someone she liked. Or, perhaps she was just trying to spare my feelings.

'Hello,' he said as he pulled up another beach bed.

'George, meet Fran,' Jess introduced us. 'You don't mind George joining us today do you Fran?'

'It's just that I've finished all my business calls and have the day spare before flying home tomorrow,' he explained. He sounded quite apologetic about it and quaintly shy.

I laughed at Jess' sorrowful face and said that of course I didn't mind.

'I hope you got some good orders,' I said.

'Indeed, we'll definitely be stocking the wine from the place I saw you both yesterday,' George answered.

'Oh good, I hope it travels well because Jess and I have become addicted to it.' And with that I settled down with my book, so they could have their own conversation.

Getting a bit bored a couple of hours later I went in for another swim and felt rather virtuous. I could feel the bloating in my tummy easing and thought I'd really be able to enjoy my evening meal. When Jess told me that she and George were going to the beach bar for some lunch I elected to stay on the bed and soak up some more sunshine. I was being very good about putting on the factor, I didn't want to burn and then need to stay in the shade. I was also developing quite a nice colour. It's so long since my legs had a decent tan. My mind kept going back to the last time I was here and the happy hours I'd spent sitting on this very beach with Pieta, Paulo and whatever girl he was courting that day.

As Jess and George wandered back to our space on the beach, I had a chance to have a real proper look at him. Not the usual sort that Jess would go for, I worried that he may get too much sun as he's a red head and covered in freckles as well. He also seemed quite short, just a few inches taller than Jess, so I thought all those high heeled shoes she had wouldn't get much use when she was with him. She usually liked her men tall dark and handsome; this was a huge departure for her. He seemed nice though and throughout the afternoon they talked and laughed and talked some more with lots more laughter. It was nice to see her so animated and happy. Although happy for my friend I couldn't help feeling a little bit jealous. If only I could have someone that I got on with so well.

My mind kept returning to Pieta. He was cold and distant with me and really didn't want me around him or his family. His mother was frigid to the point of rudeness since that first night but why would that be? I was no-one special in her son's life. What could have got into her? She'd been so easy to talk to on the plane but since then she – well, what can I say?

These thoughts were going through my head all afternoon, I hadn't even read a page of the book I'd brought with me. I finished the coke that Jess and George had brought back from the bar for me and looked at the sea. Well at least I had broken one of the memories today. Of four young people splashing and frolicking in the sea. Those visions kept popping into my head bringing a sadness I didn't want to feel. This holiday was supposed to be a healing trip after my emotional divorce. That wasn't going to work was it? Well, I reasoned not if I let it become sad. Time for that virtual steel rod.

When Jess had said a long lingering goodbye to George, she told me that it was time we went in to get changed. I realised that as I had been reliving my memories all afternoon it was getting quite late. As we walked back to the hotel Jess told me. 'George is divorced with two nearly grown children. He is forty-three years old and runs his own wine importing business. I just thought I might as well tell you all about him so that you don't have to ask questions.'
I smiled and said I was happy for her, he seemed nice. 'I expect he gets quite lonely on these trips. What score did you give him, when you first saw him?'

'Only a five, actually but it rose to a ten by the time we landed and got off the plane.'

'And now?'

'Off the scale. In a league of his own.'

It was obvious that this was not the last I was going to hear about George but for now Jess decided she'd given me enough information. I think my friend has fallen in love and I'll have difficulty in changing the subject for the next few days. Oh well at least I won't have much time to think about Pieta and how to get to talk to him. Jess' phone pinged, Oh what a surprise a text from George. So, I went for my shower to give her some space.

Oh dear! I'll have to wear another bikini tomorrow to

blend in the strap marks that have appeared. I can't in all honesty think that I will be showing it off much when I get home, but I might as well keep it as even as possible. I also noticed that my blond hair was already about three shades lighter. It really showed up the green of my eyes. So tonight, just a flash of mascara, a smear of lipstick and that's me done.
When we were both dressed Jess suggested that instead of eating in the hotel restaurant that we take a stroll along the sea front to find another place to have our dinner.

'Good idea,' I said, I wasn't looking forward to being snubbed my Mrs. Bianchi again. Best to stay out of her way. We managed to exit the hotel without encountering her, thank goodness. The evening was warm and as we ambled along the road looking at likely places to eat, we stopped to read the menu of one place. All seafood. 'Hmm sounds nice,' Jess said.

'Ladies come on in, you will not get better food in Rimini.' Called a voice from inside the restaurant. Paulo! Have this family taken over the whole of Rimini?

'Shall we?' Asked Jess looking at the apprehension that just plastered itself on my face.

'Might as well, in for a penny, in for a pound,' I answered her. Taking a deep breath, time for that steel rod. Just to break my mood I asked Jess where that saying was from.

'Something to do with being in debt, I think if you owe money you may as well owe a pound as a penny. It's still owed.'

'Okay, that makes sense. Jess' hobby of studying where saying and phrases came from was not only entertaining but served the purpose of breaking into my damaging mind set. 'You're constant source of useless information.'

'Well better than being boring.'

Having settled at a small table on the outside balcony area we asked for a glass of nice cold wine and perused the menu again. Well, Paulo was nearly right. The food was delicious, if not the best in Rimini it was definitely a contender for top spot. Listening to Jess's monologue regarding the delectable George, I didn't notice Paulo sit down next to me until it was too late.

'He loved you, you know. He wrote to you many letters. But heard nothing back.'

I stared at him in confusion.

'Letters? He wrote to me? I never got any letters.'

'No? So many he wrote, for many months after you went home.'

I shook my head and felt close to tears. Where's that steel rod when you really need it? I can't cry again. I won't.

'Ahh, well, no matter. You are married I see. All long ago, many years have passed.' Glancing down at my left hand and with a sad shake of his head he got up and went into the restaurant, before I could say another word.

Jess looked at me.

'Well that would explain Mother Bianchi's attitude.'

I looked down at the offending ring and wondered what to do. I already have a white mark under it so was taking it off really an option? Replace it with another ring? But will I ever get close enough to Pieta to explain anyway? Not with his formidable mother around all the time. But to admit that I had been married and was now divorced? How would that go down? Probably just as badly.

'Just take it off, you'll soon brown up underneath it,' Jess told me.

'Do you think so?' I said sipping it off and putting it safely in my purse. I felt so liberated, and free. I'd not noticed just how much I'd been clinging to my now dead marriage. But without the ring I could almost see my shoulders relaxing, and feel the tension leaving my body. I wondered how long it would take for the white mark to go and the wasting in my finger to fill out. That ring had been there for so long and I kept looking at my now nude finger. That was it, the last thing I had to do to admit to myself that I was now alone. No husband. No children, just me. I had taken one more and this time, final step away from Ray and my marriage. But Paulo said that Pieta had written to me. He had sent many letters. I never received a single letter from him. How could that be? I know when we went home that time everything was overshadowed by Mum and Dad splitting up. But Mum and I didn't move to a new house for quite some time so if letters came, I should have got them.

Jess went to the counter to pay the bill and I saw her talking to Paulo. They seemed to be in conversation far too long to just be paying the bill. He looked at me and smiled. Well at least one member of the family could bring themselves to be friendly.

We walked back to the hotel and saw a large limo outside the front. Mrs. Bianchi was supervising the packing of her bags in the boot and Guilia stood with her.

'She's going to Guilia's house for the rest of her holiday. Paulo told me,' Jess said.

'Oh, that's what the big conversation was about,' I said.

'More or less,' she said mysteriously.

How did I feel about that? Relieved and sad at the same time. I had some serious thinking to do. So, as we were sitting on our balcony drinking our night cap glass of wine and Jess talked about George, I went into my own mind and had a good look at my feelings.

Was I heartbroken at Ray leaving me? Not so much as I thought I'd be. I'm still very angry with him though. All my sadness is based around the fact that I waited so long for him to qualify and start his business. I supported him emotionally and financially through all that time. Waiting until we were comfortably off while my body clock was ticking along ever faster. Waiting until I could have the family I longed for. Only for him to have that very family with another woman. I'd continued to work in the graphic design studio, gaining all the qualifications I could. Now I work freelance and earn good money. Ray signed the house over to me when he left and paid off the mortgage. Saying it's only fair. He was never tight with the money, always generous. I'm comfortably off and even have some savings or did before the studio was built. I am free. I thought, free of all the baggage. Independent, free and single. Single and alone. That's me.

I slept well that night and even woke up with a smile, it's so long since I did that. Due to the fact I think that I'd removed the last vestige of my marriage, my ring. That had taken such a weight off my shoulders. Standing on the balcony waiting for Jess to finish her text conversation with George, I noticed that Pieta's car was not in its usual place. Perhaps he had work to do at the vineyard and would be in later. I was looking forward to a leisurely breakfast as we were going on a trip around the historic parts of Rimini today. Another coach, some super architecture and places of huge religious significance. Jess also found some shops via the internet on her phone, but their clothes were going to be too expensive for us. Nice to look though. And pretend. A new concept, virtual must haves.

Pieta still hadn't arrived at the hotel as we boarded the bus to take us on our excursion. And I noted that he wasn't parked up in his usual spot when we arrived back. I was beginning to worry that I wouldn't see him again before we went home. We only had two more days. Jess was very happy about that as she was looking forward to seeing George again. She'd arranged for him to meet us at the airport and drive us home. I was just longing to see Pieta. Now I knew what the trouble was with his mother I wanted to talk to him and explain that I had never received his letters. Would my life have been so very different? Would I have married Ray? Or would I be an Italian wife with a bunch of children by now? How did he feel about me now? Probably he'd just got on with his life and put me to the back of his mind. The only times I've seen him he's been distant, cold and unfriendly, apart from at his farm. But of course, we'd not been together long enough for me to gauge his feeling for me.

The last two days of our holiday we stayed by the pool. Jess knew I was longing to see Pieta and wouldn't want to miss an opportunity by going down to the beach. Just in case he put in an appearance. On our last night we went again to Paulo's restaurant in the hope of seeing him, but he was not there either. They must all be holidaying with their mother. I could feel panic setting up inside me. I really wanted to see Pieta and put him straight about my broken marriage and about not getting his letters. But it was not to be.

Chapter 8

Fran

We went home, and I didn't see Pieta again. My heart was heavy as we drove home from the airport, but Jess was so happy to be with George. I couldn't begrudge her this happiness; I was sitting in the back of his car listening to them talking happily and feeling downright jealous. I tried to be happy and join in the conversation when I was expected too but Jess could see that I had other things on my mind. All I could think of was the wasted opportunity of being with Pieta and the love that I realised I still felt for him. But I had lost him all over again.

When I got indoors, I just tipped my bag out in the utility room next to the washing machine. Put the first load in and went to look at my poor overgrown garden with the new structure. Who was that ringing the doorbell? I opened the door and there was Ray. Well at least he didn't try to walk straight in. Although as I've had the locks changed, he couldn't.

'Any chance of a coffee? I've brought fresh milk.' Opening the door wide to let him in I smelled that familiar aftershave on him. It was comforting, but that I realised now, was the theme of our marriage. That it was comfortable. There never was much in the way of passion between us. Maybe that's why he left me for Samantha.

'Fran, did you have a good holiday?' Wrapping his arms around me. I just froze in his embrace. We have never been very tactile. Hugs were never high on our agenda while we were married. Perhaps marriage to the delectable Sam had changed him.

'Yes, it was really nice to get some warmth and sunshine. Jess enjoyed herself as well,' I answered.

Slithering out of his arms and wondering why he was here and where this was going. But perhaps he was just being friendly. 'How's Sam and the baby?'

'Hmm, she's great and he throws up all the time,' He grimaced. I couldn't help myself and had to say.

'Perhaps you left it a bit late to be having children?' I saw a spark of annoyance cross his face, but he soon hid it and smiled.

'Have you decided on a name for the baby yet? Last I heard you were having a problem agreeing.'

'Sam wants to call him Dylan and I thought Oscar would be better. So, we compromised on Dylan Oscar Middleton. It's growing on me and I think it's quite distinguished.'

'Dyl, for short? Or Dom?' I asked.

'Oh no, I don't think we'll shorten it. I'd like to keep it as it is.'

'Oh, yeah, like that's going to happen. All names get shortened.'

'Not my son,' he said in mock severity. At least I think it was mock. But then again, that spark of annoyance which was quickly hidden. It did occur to me that he would normally be at work right now and why was he taking time out to bring me milk? He wanted to say something but seemingly he bottled out of doing so because he drank his coffee down and said.

'Anyway, must be off, Thanks for the coffee.'

'Thanks for the milk,' I said.

'I should have brought you some bread as well, I know what it's like coming home to a house with no food,' he said ruefully.

'Don't worry, it's early days for Sam, she'll be up to speed soon and get the shopping in.'

'HA!' he said but again quickly hid the fact that he

was annoyed about something.

Then he went to his car and drove off. What was that all about? Ray hadn't been friendly for months, in fact all the while we were going through the divorce, he could hardly say a polite word to me. Well, I thought, so much for a relaxing holiday. It has done nothing but bring back memories that were best forgotten. I went to sit on the sofa and had a good weep. Was I crying for Pieta? For Ray? For me? Or more for all the wasted time. Maybe I'm just tired I thought as I dried my eyes and went to re-do my makeup. I took a quick look at my emails and decided that I needed one more day before I got back to work. There's nothing urgent there. Although, working at home as I did, I could do it any time. I noted down the times of some client visits next week.

While I'd been away the builders had been as good as their word and they've finished off the studio. I've always done my design work upstairs in one of the larger bedrooms but found that a bit restricting. Especially if customers wanted to visit to discuss changes to their work in progress. It felt uncomfortable to be taking smart suited businessmen up to the personal area of my house. Especially now that I was living alone here. I'd discussed it with Dad, and we had come up with the idea of the studio in the garden. My clients or customers could come to look at their designs without ever having to come into the house. I found out I was allowed to do this under permitted development, and it was nearly finished. All painted and there were just a few bits of furniture still up in the bedroom that I needed to move. I'm very satisfied with the look of it. Back to work now, no more procrastinating. The holiday's over and for the next few days I was very strict with myself concentrating on the work and getting used to my new workspace. And try to bring some order to my poor beleaguered garden.

'Mum, are you in later? I'll pop in for a cuppa after I've done a bit of shopping,' I said when I phoned my mother and simultaneously wrote a shopping list. I somehow need to find a way to ask her about these letters. But I know she's vulnerable and still a bit sad that her and Dad broke up all those years ago. She's now convinced herself that he was the love of her life. Dad is remarried and very happy, but Mum was, it would seem, waiting for him to see the error of his ways and come back to her. It always seemed odd to me that she should set so much store by being married to him. Looking back on their marriage it was always turbulent and a kind of peace settled over them for a while after they split. That is of course until Dad met Sheila. Then it was as if, although Mum obviously didn't want him, no-one else should have him.

'Have you been to see your Dad?' she asked as I walked in the door. Still a bit jealous of any time I spent with him.

'Not since I got home, no. They're still away for another week or so, anyway.'

'Oh, okay. So how was Rimini? Changed much over the years?'

'Yes, it's changed a lot, huge hotels and the sea front's more or less full up now. Do you remember where we stayed? There's a big new hotel there and Jess and I stayed just two blocks away from it.'

'Well you are looking nice and tanned; it must have been warm. Ray came to see me the other day. He looks a sad sight. I think he regrets leaving you. You could have him back you know, instead of being alone.'

'Yes, he came to see me.'

'And?'

'We had a coffee, that's all. He's a Dad and has a lovely young wife. I'm glad. He's a family man now and I've resigned myself to being childless. Never going to happen for me, is it?'

With a sigh Mum said, 'Never say never my darling, and he isn't. Happy that is. He's erm troubled.'

I just shook my head not wanting to discuss Ray and thought that I should come right out with it and tell her why I could never contemplate taking him back.

'I met Pieta while I was there. And Paulo, do you remember the two Ps as Dad called them?'

'Oh, that Italian lad you thought you were in love with. He's still working there during the summer, is he?'

'Yes and no. He owns the hotel Jess and I stayed in. Paulo said that Pieta wrote to me when I came home. But I never saw any letters from him.'

The surprised look on Mum's face faded into a wary expression and she couldn't look me in the eye. I knew she was hiding something from me, changing the subject to try and steer me away from talk of those letters.

'Well you have a lovely colour. Not too many strap marks I hope.' It was one of Mum's things whenever she went on holiday that she should not get strap marks. How would that look when wearing her posh ball gowns with white lines across her shoulders?

'Yes, it was just right, not too hot to sit out in and sunny all the time.'

'And you say this George that Jess met is bringing some of that wine you liked over here?'

'He was doing a reconnaissance trip to find Italian wines to import. Jess talked to him on the plane.'

'Oh, you couldn't sit together?'

'No, we were separated, I was seated next to a nice Italian woman. Pieta's mother in fact. Stop all this Mum. Where there any letters from Italy for me when we came home from that holiday?' Was that actual fear I saw on her face now? What was she hiding?

'Oh, oh yes, there were some I believe, that arrived from Italy, if I remember right, but what with the divorce from your father, I forgot all about them. I was so upset at the time and I just couldn't think straight. I think I might've kept them. I think I put them somewhere safe. They may be in one of those boxes in the loft. I don't remember, it was a long time ago. I'm not sure if I can lay hands on them.' She was acting so vague and that more than anything told me the truth.

My blood ran cold. How could she be so dismissive of the love I had for Pieta? Just because I was only eighteen and not to be considered grown up? I know now that I still love him, and I have lost him again. I have to know if he had any feeling for me at all. From the evidence last week, it would seem that he didn't. But now armed with the knowledge that he'd written it was important that I find those letters if I possibly could. Maybe she could have saved me all that heart ache. If she hadn't interfered and kept his letters from me. I was so angry with her I nearly walked out of the house there and then. But I had to find those letters, if she still had them. She waffled on some more about what a hard time she had when their marriage broke up. How she was in a state of misery and confusion. That she may have kept his letters but really everything then was such a muddle that she really didn't know. I got up from her couch and headed upstairs.

'Where are you going?' she asked desperately.

'To get my letters if they're in your loft,' I answered from halfway up the stairs. I pulled down the loft hatch and the ladder and climbed up into the vast dusty space. There were loads of boxes there. Full of stuff she had claimed was hers from the family home. She'd never even opened most of them since she lived in this house. Full of memories of my childhood and my parents' marriage. Why had she laid claim to them if she really didn't want them? Stored for future use. Like her so-called love for my dad.
She followed me up the ladder and immediately pointed to one quite small box.

'That one,' she said knowing all along where they were.

I took the box downstairs to the lounge. And we opened it. There were a lot of letters in there, and her wedding head dress. Pictures I had painted as a child. Cards from their wedding and her blue garter, the elastic a bit perished now. Photos of Dad and herself when they were younger and first married. Some of me as a baby. All smiling to the camera. I looked up to her and saw the tears starting to run down her cheeks. From being angry with her I felt genuinely sad. Maybe I'd been mistaken, and she really did love Dad. As if reading my thoughts, she looked into my eyes and said.

'Yes, my love. I've always loved your Dad. I know I went about things all wrong when we split, and I really think if I'd been less angry and more giving, I could have saved our marriage. It's my biggest regret and I have to live with it.'

I hugged her. She's a very complex woman, my Mum.

'Oh Mum,' I said thinking that I have to put the anger aside. I just felt that I should go away from her and cool down but for all her faults she is my mother. Hard as it was at this moment I had to once again hide my feelings. Why do other people allow their anger to show and seem to gain some satisfaction from it? I can always see the other persons point of view and however angry I might feel I'm frightened to let it show. She pulled out a pile of airmail letters that were hidden right down the bottom of the box.

   'Here, these are yours and I know I should've given them to you. I was so afraid of losing you as well. I knew if you got those you would end up in Italy. I was selfish and wanted you here with me.'

   'That's why you were so immediately accepting of Ray? Even though I knew you were both worried that I was working while he studied?'

   'At least he is English, and you wouldn't be in another country,' She said nodding. 'I knew I'd lost your Dad and couldn't bear the thought of you going as well. Leaving me here all alone'

Oh goodness, how do I cope with that? I now have no-one to be angry with, she was just so needy, and I could nearly understand why she kept the letters from me, although as she said, it was selfish of her. But she is my Mother and I love her for all her faults, her hysterical outbursts and all the scheming to get Dad back.

 'I still wonder how you could have hidden these from me, I was old enough to make up my own mind. Maybe I wouldn't have gone to Italy, maybe we wouldn't have got together anyway. You were so happy for me to marry Ray but look what happened there? He upped and left. Now I am alone and have only memories of a marriage and a long-lost love,' despite my sympathy for her, my resentment was building up again.   'Did Dad know these had arrived?'

   'I don't believe so, no. He'd only have encouraged

you, and I - I would have been left lonely,' she sighed.

'Well, now I am on my own and you stopped me from knowing what would have happened. I was obviously not Ray's only love, was I? Now it's too late for Pieta and me.'

'It's never too late for you, there's someone out there just waiting for the right time. Ray isn't happy you know. He regrets what he did. He is basically a good man and you could do worse.'

I was so shocked that she would even think this way.

'No, no, never. I've been there and worked my socks off to make a good life for us and he just threw it back in my face. I will never have him back. Don't even go there Mum. It isn't going to happen. Once bitten by the Ray viper, twice shy.'

'Well, that's a shame, at least you wouldn't be alone.'

'There are worse things than being alone, Mum. Being dumped, for one. Just because you couldn't get over your split from Dad and spent so many years harking after your old life, doesn't mean I'm the same. I have more pride.'

'Well, all I can say is, don't let pride stop you from having a good life.'

'And having a man who has proved he can't be loyal and faithful is having a good life?'

'You may meet someone else; you know. Someone who can make you happy,' she said, changing tactic.

'Yes, I very well may, but not if Ray's hanging around.'

'It's never too late, never,' she said again as she got up and went to answer the front doorbell. She opened it to a man who was smartly dressed and in his mid-fifties. He had distinguished closely cut steel grey hair and a beard which was also very nicely trimmed. He was a few inches taller than Mum which isn't difficult as she is a shorty.

'This is Michael,' she said. 'Michael this is my daughter, Fran.'

Well that's a turn up for the books. Mum has a boyfriend at last. It only took some twelve years or so to get over the loss of her marriage. Still seething and just wanting to get away but I had to stay and meet this person.

'Hello Michael, nice to meet you. I'd like to say I know all about you, but I know absolutely nothing of you,' I noted that my voice was tart and bitter. Although I tried to sound friendly, but the anger was still bubbling up in me.

'I know quite a lot about you though Fran, your Mum never stops telling me how perfect you are.' He said with a smile both to me and to Mum. She preened a bit and slapped his arm affectionately. I just wanted to go away then but felt obliged to stay for a while. It would have been rude to walk out as soon as he came in.

We sat down and had quite a long conversation. Even though I was desperate to get home and read my letters. I found out how they had met and how long they'd been together. That he had a house not far away and that they were contemplating moving in together. I must say I was a bit shocked that I knew nothing of all this. I know I had been caught up in my own troubles quite a bit but surely, I should have seen that Mum looked so different and happier. How could I still be angry with her when it became pointedly clear that I had been thinking only about myself all this time. Maybe I was the selfish one. But she's not alone now, is she? And I am. All alone. Although I had never met Michael before they apparently have known each other for many years, but only got together recently.

Eventually it was time for me to politely leave so that I could go home and read Pieta's letters. I said my goodbyes and invited them both over for Sunday lunch. Michael, said that was very nice but why didn't I join them for Sunday roast at the pub down the road? Sounds good to me so we agreed to meet at 12 o'clock. I hoped by that time I would've calmed down a bit.

I drove home, but how I managed to get there with those letters burning a hole in my bag, I don't know. I was dying to read them. As I walked in the door, lugging my bags of shopping, my phone started ringing, and I looked to see who was calling. Ray. I didn't want to talk to him right now. I wanted to sit with a glass of wine and read my letters. But I accepted the call.

'Ray, what can I do for you?'

'Just making sure you're okay,' he answered. 'I'd love to pop round again. We could go out for a bite to eat if you like.'

'I'm not sure that's a good idea Ray, let me think about it.' He was about to talk again when I cut the call. A bit curt and rude, not like me at all. But I didn't need him hanging around complicating things, I need time and space. I certainly didn't want him piling his own problems on me. Not right now. Then my phone sang its jolly tune again and I was all ready to give him a mouthful of abuse when I saw that it was Jess calling. With the phone to my ear I wandered into the kitchen and poured a very large glass of white wine.

'I hear glugging, but I bet it isn't our Italian wine,' she said.

'Ha ha, no, it's supermarket best,' I told her.

'Well, George has secured a contract to bring some over, so we can indulge in it very soon.'

'Does he have to go out and sign contracts or will it all

be done electronically?'

'Yes, he's going over for a quick trip. Wish I could go with him. I need more sunshine, it's cold here.' Glancing out of the kitchen window at the blue sky and sunny day I wondered how cold she was feeling. but then again, I have three layers of clothing on now we're home.

'Oh, so George is going to import Pieta's wine, and any others?'

'He hopes so, but apparently the blend of grapes Pieta can grow is just right for the English market. So, George says any way. There are a few others he's interested in, but Pieta's are the ones he wants to get here as soon as possible.'

'Oh good, I'm looking forward to buying some of that.'

'Yeah, George says it'll be the catalyst for putting him on the map as an international wine dealer.'

'So, into big business then. How long will he be gone? You're going to miss him.'

'Well, as he lives a few miles away we still don't get to see each other as much as we would like anyway. But if he can secure this contract, he is thinking of opening another distribution centre in Bishops Stortford. He'll then relocate, here near us.'

'Oh, wow. You too have got close then?'

'Yes, it's all happened rather quickly, but let's face it none of us are getting any younger, are we?'

'No, you're right. Even Mum. Mum has a new boyfriend.'

'What? Wow I didn't think she would ever contemplate someone else. She had been so fixed on your Dad for so long.'

'They seem very happy together.'

'Did you ask her about those letters?'

'I have them all here and was just going to open them and read them accompanied by this glass of wine.'

'I'm coming over, with more wine,' Jess said as she cut the call.

Twenty minutes later she walked in to find me in floods of tears. I'd read the first two letters and I was so full of emotion and sadness at what I'd missed out on. I couldn't go any further at the moment. The love Pieta had felt for me was all in these letters in his broken English. I cried for the loss and waste of time. His love poured off the pages and if I'd got them when they'd been posted I'd have been able to write back to him, sending all the love I felt for him. My heart's breaking again. How many times can one heart break? It seems it can go on breaking into infinity.

He wasn't just another Italian boy looking for a quick lay, he had fallen in love just as I had. We should have been together all this time and now it's too late. He thought I had strung him along all those years ago and that I'd come home to forget him. I could see his heart break in those letters.

I showed them to Jess and she was shocked at the emotion that poured out of them. We cried together. And drank more wine than was good for either of us. Then I let my anger boil over. I ranted and shouted about how unfair it all was and how selfish my mother had been. The wine was fuelling this rant, and Jess just stayed sitting on my sofa and listened while I shouted and paced frantically around the living room.

'Maybe, just maybe I'd have been living in Italy all this time with a man that really loved me and one who I really loved. How could she do that? How could she be so selfish. I might have had children by now and she put a stop to that. Hiding these letters from me. I came home and just put him aside thinking that he was just another Italian waiter who collected English girls addresses. Trophy hunting. But he wasn't, was he? He had love for me and now it's too late. He thinks I am married and settled and that I was just another sluttish English girl who strings boys along for the fun of it.'

Sitting there listening to all this Jess let me rant and when I was exhausted and finally sat down, she wrapped her arms around me and let me cry. I seem to have been able to get rid of most of the terrible rage now. I could begin to see Mum's point of view and wondered what I'd have done if it had been me. Would I have hidden the letters? Knowing that my only daughter may fly away because of them? Having just lost her marriage I accepted that she'd been feeling vulnerable and faced the possibility of loneliness. But now she has Michael and who do I have?

'His mother was just as bad when we were there though, wasn't she? She whisked him away before you too had a chance to talk properly. As soon as she saw that you were the one that he loved, she hid him,' Jess reasoned.

'He didn't have to go though, did he? Is that what mothers do?' Protect themselves by hurting their children?'

'Not all mothers but you can see how it would be for them to think they may lose their children.'

'I suppose I can understand her point of view and I just have to swallow it up and get on with my life. What's done is done and I can't undo it. Oh, by the way, she is trying to get me and Ray back together. He went to see her and told her he's not happy with Sam and the kid is getting on his nerves. He thinks I will just jump through his hoop and take him back. All the time I was round there this afternoon she was hinting that I'll end up lonely. He came around here with milk and asked for a coffee, the day we got home. I hadn't even unpacked. He keeps popping in and ringing, then just before you phoned, he asked me out for a meal.'

'Oh, good grief, and how do you feel about that?'

'Used, and of no consequence so long as Mum's happy thinking I'm settled, and Ray is happy getting his own way.'

'Are you going out with him then?'

'I will, just to let him know that there is no chance whatever of him insinuating himself back into my life. He burnt his bridges with me that day he walked out.' I looked at Jess questionably, she knew I was looking for an explanation of the phrase. It's just one of the things we do.

'That's something to do with the military. Retreating armies would burn bridges so the enemy couldn't follow them.'

'Oh, Well I'm certainly not going to chase after Ray. You know what? I wasn't heart broken when he went. I was just so angry at the effort I'd put into that marriage and he felt it was of no consequence, that he could just walk away. I blamed myself for so long, thinking I'd not made enough effort, that I hadn't given enough to him. But I just turned into a door mat for him to walk all over.'

Jess poured the last of the wine and we chinked glasses.

'To our new lives. And no more burned bridges.'

'Oh, I'm so sorry I have been moaning about my mixed-up life and haven't asked about George. Are you all loved up?'

A smile blossomed on Jess' face as she said. 'You know? I think I am.'

Chapter 9
Pieta

By the time I managed to get away from Mamma at Guilia's house and come back to the hotel I had missed Fran. That had obviously been Mamma's plan, to keep me hidden away. Each day I said I needed to get back, but she had kept me busy and with some of her own special emotional blackmail she wept and clung to me when I said I had to go.

'You are always so busy, when do I get a chance to be with my special one? I fly all the way from England to be with my family and you want to just pop off? Poof?' Then yesterday she just said. 'Alright, I know you have work to do,' and said goodbye to me.

Of course, Fran's holiday was finished, and she had gone home. I'd never got the chance to talk to her. I had to know if she had received my letters and if she had why had she not answered. Even just one, to let me down gently, but nothing came. Her friend Jess had apparently been very surprised to learn from Paulo that there had been letters so, maybe she didn't get them? Am I wishful thinking here? She'd gone home and got married. Did she really not love me back then? I was so sure at the time that we felt the same and we would find a way to be together. We had it planned. She would finish her college course and set up as a designer here in Italy. Now she could do it with all the internet and such it would be easy for her to re-locate.

But she was back in England. I don't have an address for her, but I did have her friends address as she had made the booking. But would I be setting myself up for another heart break? Should I just carry on and try once again to forget her? I remember that her Father had been quite friendly, but her Mother had been distinctly cold toward me. No, I had to forget and her bury myself in my work. And maybe let Mamma have her way and find me a nice Italian girl to marry and have children with.

But work, work was what kept me going before. Work, work and more work and getting rich. But being rich means nothing if you have no one to share it with. And not just anyone.

'You should find a wife,' my mother constantly told me. 'You will end up a lonely rich old man. You need a wife to give you many children.'

I've loved once but could I bring myself to try again? I had to stop letting my thoughts drift to Fran and our time together.

No, what I really needed to do now is find out if I was actually able to export my wine to England. George Hampton of Hampton wine importers was coming out again to see me and I really needed to concentrate on the wine production. He'd want to know how much we could produce each year and many other things. I needed to be getting some figures together for him. This was a great opportunity for me and my wines. I wondered if I could get to England as well. Which lead my mind back to Fran. Oh, Fran, how could an eighteen-year-old boy fall so madly in love? Or was It as Mamma said, just that she got away and I was shutting my heart to any others in fear of being hurt again?

I had to settle down to work on those figures and they made me smile looking at the amounts the vineyard was putting out. Very satisfying to know that all my hard work was coming to fruition.

'Riches are all well and good but there is going to come a time when you need company to share it with, children to hand it on to,' Bella told me. Perhaps I should just forget Fran, I thought, and let Mamma find me a wife.

Chapter 10

Fran

Putting all thoughts of my holiday aside I had to settle back into work. There were clients to see and new jobs to sort out. There's an email from one of my existing customers who wanted to see me regarding a new brand they were setting up, they needed logos and point of sale material designed. Well that'll keep me busy for a few weeks and hopefully that would take my mind off Pieta and the fact that George was going back, where I so wanted to be. At least we'll be able to buy Pieta's wine in England very soon if George can get that contract sorted out with him.

I must stop myself from thinking of the Bacchus Hotel and concentrate on my job. I still have to earn a living and I can't let thoughts of past times interfere with my work. There are customers who look to me to design for them, and I have a reputation to keep up. I could always give Jess a letter for George to deliver to Pieta, but he would just probably send it straight back. He obviously didn't want anything to do with me now, he made that clear by avoiding us while Jess and I were in Italy. Apart, from that one time.

I've also to set about putting the rest of my design equipment into the new studio. Now that all the expenses are accounted for and I can just concentrate on getting it all set up and actually do some work. It was a hard slog dealing with planners, building control, and builders, but It's there now and what with having floor covering down and the decorating done I can get to it. I used the capital from my divorce that I'd put aside, to invest in this new workplace and in myself. I need to let everything else go right now and not think any more about Pieta. Or the letters. Or our love. Our lost love.

Then there's Ray. He's visited quite often since that first day, when he brought milk. Why was he spending so much time here with me when he had a young wife at home and even younger son? In fact, I'm supposed to be meeting him for dinner tonight. I'd tried to find an excuse, but he said we had things to talk about. Now we are officially divorced, and Ray is even married again I really can't see what there is to talk about. And what was he saying to Sam every time he was here? He'd lied to me once and now it seemed he was more than likely lying to Sam. He's probably telling her he had to stay late at work. I get the sneaky feeling that he was still getting encouragement from Mother, as well. Mum hated the idea that Pieta was back in my thoughts even if he isn't back in my life. After all she'd kept his letters hidden all this time. What would have happened if I'd received those letters? How different would my life had been? Would I still be in love with Pieta or would the relationship have run its course?

Because our relationship was cut off in infancy, does that make the heart break I'm now feeling stronger? Would we have made it as a couple? We were both only eighteen. Can you find the love of your life at eighteen? He's a good-looking man and should be married with children. Although his mother said he had never married. Why was that? Because he worked too hard? Or did he work to forget me?

No, I wasn't a big deal in his life, just a bit of skirt to flirt with. I know no more about him now than I did back then. Was I really in love with him or just the thought of him? Being with Ray had been exciting at first but it soon became hard work. As the only wage earner for several years while he took his degree and when he first started his company, he didn't bring much home. Luckily the business thrived. Then I was able to step back and become a freelance designer. I'd built a good client base by then.

That was my plan, to work from home, still bring in some money to the household and have room in my life for a child, our child. But Ray had resisted having children until his business was stable and he was earning more.

'Perhaps we should wait a little longer, I want children as much as you Fran, but the thought of struggling for money again scares me. I just want my earning to be secure before you stop work.'

'But I can still work, from home? And look after a baby.'

'I still think we should wait for a while, just to make sure. We've got a big mortgage here. I have loans to pay off. When the business loans are all paid, we can think about a family.'

I thought that was sensible at the time and had gone along with it even though I was yearning for a baby. But then Ray had become a father and left me for Sam, and my world crashed and burned around my ears. Mother urged me to forgive and forget. Try to save my marriage at all costs, but I was so hurt and angry by what Ray had done. I couldn't just forgive him. But then again, Mother had spent quite a few years trying to regain what she had with Dad. Now, even she'd moved on and was happy with Michael. Dad was happy with his wife Sheila; Ray should've been happy with Sam and their baby. Jess was happy with George. And then there was me, alone and thinking of a lost love and so much lost time.

Talking of time, I rushed to get ready to meet Ray. I

wasn't not sure what to wear. He'd be dressed up to the nines as I expect he'd told Sam that this was a business meeting. I didn't want to be too casual, but I on the other hand didn't feel I should dress up for this occasion. I don't want to give him ideas that I was making too much of an effort for his sake. So, one of my new silk blouses and jeans with high heeled sandals. Yes, that sounded good. He said he'd pick me up, but I said I'd rather meet him there. I wanted to be able to leave under my own steam if it got too heavy. There could be plenty of things he wanted to talk about, money, perhaps he wants to cut my dividend now he has a child. Or he probably wants to buy my shares of his business from me. We both invested to start it up. He could be having another child with Sam. But Dylan Oscar is still only a few months old so that's unlikely. My mind's full of things Ray might need to talk about. There was only one way to find out. That's go and talk with him.

Chapter 11

Fran

'You look gorgeous.' Ray said as I sat down.

'Thank you. You look alright yourself as always. New suit?' I answered as he poured me some wine.

'This is rather a nice Italian wine, thought it would remind you of your holiday,' he said putting the bottle back in the cool bucket.

'Well, that makes sense as we're in an Italian restaurant. How are things going with the baby?'

'Oh, he grows so fast, but it'll be nice when he sleeps through the night. How do people manage when they have loads of kids keeping them awake all night?'

'Well that's not something I'd know much about,' I answered.

He had the grace to look a bit shamefaced at that comment. He is a handsome man, his brown hair swept back from his face and his hazel eyes looking rather tired. Yes, I could see why I fell for his charms. He always could charm the birds from the trees and I'm sure that is why he's so successful with the business.

After we'd eaten, and I had refused a second glass of wine on the grounds that I was driving home, I was sipping a coffee when I asked him why we were here.

'You said there was something you wanted to talk about?'

He poured himself another glass of wine, took a deep breath and said.

'I've made the biggest mistake of my life. Fran I should never have left you. I don't love Sam and the baby is just getting on my nerves. I really want us to start again and I know you've not got another lover or anything, so I thought I could move back in with you? We could have a lovely life and I really would make a go of it this time. I hurt you I know but I can make up for that. What do you say? Can I come home?' he reached across the table to try and hold my hand which I snatched away as if I'd just received a huge electric shock.

I was so stunned that I just stayed in my seat with my mouth hanging open. Then I put down my coffee cup, picked up my bag, stood up and walked out of the restaurant without saying another word. To say I was angry would be putting it mildly. I was furious. How dare he? How could he just come out with it so blatantly? He had just bundled in and not in his usual charming way but like the proverbial bull in the rather nice china shop. I was so shocked at his attitude. Did he really think I would jump back into his arms just like that? With that cheeky, arrogant selfish attitude. How come I attract all these selfish people around me? And if baby Dylan was getting on his nerves now, what does that say about me wanting a family. If
I was fool enough to take him back, would he still try to make me wait for children until I'm too old. Anyway, I know now I don't love him. Probably never did.

He couldn't follow me out straight away as he had to pay the bill before he left the restaurant and I got to my car before I caught sight of him rushing out. I had to drive past him, and he stood in the road trying to wave me down. Oh no. I thought as I swerved round him. No. No. I made myself drive a bit more steadily but all the time thinking. How could he possibly think I would go back to him? After what he had done? How could I ever trust him again? And there was extra baggage now in the form of a tiny baby. Did he really think so little of me that he thought I would fall straight back into his arms and forgive what he had done? What does that say about his feeling for his wife and child? Mother! I know she had something to do with this, was encouraging him.

Pulling up outside Mum's house I could see she had company. Michael was there. I stayed in the car for a few minutes trying to calm myself before I went in. Oh, if only I'd taken notice of the calming techniques of all those yoga classes Jess dragged me to. Deep breathing. After all I can't just go in there and accuse her of interfering.

Feeling a bit calmer, I went in. I didn't knock as I never had done so. But Mum was surprised to see me.

'Oh, Fran. I thought you were…um…'.

'Out with my ex-husband?' I finished her sentence for her, the anger bubbling up again.

'Yes, I saw Ray and he mentioned it,' she said regaining her composure.

'I'll bet you did. And you'll know which restaurant we went to as well, you also know why he wanted to go there, and you probably encouraged him.'

Michael got up taking in everything I was saying. 'Your Mum just doesn't want you to be lonely,' he said.

I had to sit down; I was suddenly exhausted. I looked at the pair of them and said.

'I've already told you Mum; I will not have Ray back. Not now, not ever. Stop trying to live my life for me. Didn't you learn your lesson as far as that went by withholding Pieta's letters? Tell you what. You live your live and let me live mine, shall we see how that goes?'

Michael Looked puzzled. 'Letters? What letters?'

'Letters that came from Pieta for me when we came home that time,' I said

So, I told Michael what Mum had done while she was weeping, not very quietly, in the corner seat. Mum can cry to order, when it suits her. He was annoyed with her I could see. I thought that I really didn't want to spoil their relationship while trying to sort out my own. I'm not sure why, maybe it was the nasty feeling in the room, but I started laughing. At least it lightened the atmosphere a bit.

'How many times has Ray been round here?' I asked. 'I very much doubt that you went to seek him out.'

'No, I didn't, he came around and said how sad he was and what a mess he had made of things. I told him to go away at first, but you know how persuasive he can be. He promised that he had learned his lesson and really wanted to be with you.'

'But he has a child, doesn't he?' Michael said. 'Or did you think Fran would take that on as well?'

'Oh gosh no, but I thought she would at least now have the chance to have one of her own. Ray loves you.'

'No, Ray is comfortable with me, I'm not sure he ever loved me, or he wouldn't have let Sam into his life. I'm not sure I ever really loved him as much as I should have. I married him rather quickly after coming home from Italy. He filled a gap and I needed that at the time.'

'So, what now for you? You'll be alone and in the prime of your life.'

Laughing I said. 'Mum, you just enjoy your life and let me get on with mine. I'll have to see Ray again and tell him that he must make his life with Sam and stop thinking the grass is greener on our side of the fence. Look after her Michael, and stop her from interfering in my life any further, would you?'

Michael went to sit next to Mum and put his arm round her shoulder.

'You, silly old bat,' he said kindly. Good, I thought I didn't want to bring a wedge between them. At least now that Michael knows what he is dealing with, he can try to hold her back a bit.

'Forgive me, Fran,' Mum said with all the histrionics of the past. Oh, she knows how to pile on the emotional blackmail when she wants to.

'Nothing to forgive, but no more interfering, alright?' Sniffing she nodded her head as if she had lost the capacity to speak. With Michael cuddling her I left them to it and drove home.

When I got home, I rang Dad. I just needed to hear a voice of reason. I hadn't had a chance to talk to him since I got back. He and Sheila had only just arrived home from their holiday.

I told him what Mum had done and about her encouraging Ray, and he laughed so loud I thought I didn't really need the phone to talk to him.

'She doesn't change, does she? But she has your wellbeing at heart you know, when she does things like that. You know all about that by now. How's Michael coping with her?'

'You know Michael?' I asked

'Not well but he's an acquaintance, you might say. He's always fancied your Mum. She just took a long while to see what a good chap he is.'

'Well, I think he'll cope. By the way I saw the two Ps in Italy.'

'They're still working there?'

'Paulo is married with three kids, but Pieta apparently isn't. But he happens to own the hotel Jess and I stayed in. Wealthy man now by all accounts. In fact, Paulo is married to one of Pieta's sisters. So not only lifelong friends but brothers now. Did you know about the letters?'

'What letters are those?'

'Pieta wrote to me when we came home. I asked Mum about them and made her give them up last week. She'd kept them all. She said she knew you and she were splitting up and didn't want me moving to Italy and leaving her alone.'

A long sigh escaped from my poor Father. 'Stupid woman. She's never learned not to interfere has she?'

'Well, I think she has now,' I said, adding 'Maybe.'

'So, what are you doing with the letters?'

'I still have some to read. It's not easy reading and seeing his desperation at not getting any replies.'

'Did you get to talk to him while you were there? So, I told Dad about the holiday and how Mrs. Bianchi had turned against me when she noticed I was a married woman.

'Get in touch with him, my darling.'

'How can I? He probably hates me now. No, I just have to get on with my life and take whatever the world has to throw at me. At least I can earn a living, and a good one.'

'Well I'm certainly not going to interfere, but I thought he was a really nice young chap and you could have done worse.'

'That's what Mum said, but that was about Ray.'

After a bit more chat, we said goodnight and I poured myself a really large glass of wine, not the good stuff of course, but supermarket wine. Then I got ready for bed. What a strange evening. At least Ray hadn't followed me home. Perhaps he got the message.

Chapter 12
Pieta

Well the appointment with Mr. Hampton went well. George, he told me to call him. We made good progress and he was impressed by the amount I was able to set aside for export. I would still need to keep some for the hotel and my Italian customers. But My wine in England? My first international sales.

'Maybe I should come to England and see the first batch go out for sale?'

'You should, and see my new distribution centre as well,' George said.

'It's a bit like watching your children test the big wide world. I could look Fran up if I can get time to get there,' I said.

I should have just left it alone but the feelings I had for Fran all those years ago came rushing back when I saw her. I feel like that eighteen-year-old kid again with my heart torn into bits and scattered into the sea. I had to know if Fran ever received my letters. If she did? Well then, I had my answer. She would have had a good laugh at my expense, and I'd feel a total fool. But if she didn't get them, why? Did she give me a false address? Did they get lost? My letters? They couldn't all have been lost in the post. But why didn't she ever write back? I had to stop thinking like this or I'd never be able to concentrate on the business deal

It was hard to concentrate but I reasoned with myself that if I don't get this done and get the deal signed, not only would I lose out on a fantastic opportunity to create an international brand, but I wouldn't have an excuse to go to England for some time. Would I have been so driven if I had married Fran? Stop now, I told myself sternly, I have to stop thinking about all that or I'll no longer be rich, and I'll still be lonely.

'Well I'm really glad I made this trip, Pieta. Your wines are going to do well in England.'

'I am also pleased to have met you George. I hope you're right. My wine, going international? Who would have thought?'

'I really want to expand my import business and your wine is one I can put some effort into,' George told me.

He knows his market and he also knew that my wine would be one of many he would be able to import. His business was growing and now that he'd found Jess, he was even more keen on getting his business to expand and go global. There was a new purpose to his being now, he told me. He had found a lovely lady to share his good fortune with and he thought himself very lucky. If he'd missed his plane as was so nearly the case, he wouldn't have been sitting next to Jess on the flight out to Italy. I found I was still sitting there musing about how easy it is to miss opportunities and not always simple enough to hit the right note. But that trip had been a classic piece of good luck for him. Good deals for his business and a new lady as well. He'd been very easy to talk to and I was really pleased for him. I liked him, and we'd be able to do good business together. I was just so envious of him as he'd be closer to Fran than I would ever be.

There was to be a lot to discuss with George, that afternoon. The blends, the grape harvest, the bottle count and the transport. My only worry was how well it would survive the journey. Some wines never taste the same and don't travel well. I know mine does well in Italy, but it's a bit of a guess how it would travel abroad. And would it be up to standard when it arrived in

England? George had taken several bottles home with him on his last visit, by means of his hold luggage. But that's a whole different scenario to bringing many litres of wine to the English market. I just hope we can produce enough for both markets.

Also, George was keen to change the labels on the bottle, he said they wouldn't be distinctive enough for English buyers. The supermarkets would want something that will stand out and they'd need to be a bit brighter to attract the end customer. I hadn't taken much notice of the labels on the bottle and agreed with George that they should have a revamp. All in all, it had been a good productive meeting, for both parties. Imports would begin in the autumn. Ready for the Christmas trade in England.

George said, 'I can get the labels done in England for you if you like or you can commission some here?'

'Oh no, George, I'll leave that to you. I make the wine but designing labels isn't a talent I possess.'

'Fair enough, I'll get them done for you.'

We shook hands on the deal and prepared to send all the paperwork to solicitors to finalise the contract. George is to join us for dinner in the hotel restaurant. Mamma is due to come tonight, and it would be good for her to meet another of my business associates. She's only been here for a quick visit this time, not like Mamma, she usually likes to stay longer if she can. I soon found out why.

'We will need another chair,' Mamma said as she made her usual theatrical entrance into the dining room. She always likes to make a grand entrance. I told her, 'I know, I have a business acquaintance coming for dinner.'

'You have someone far more important coming for

dinner my son. Meet Maria. She is the daughter of my old friend Mrs. Watson, from England.'

'Your old friend? Have I ever heard of this particular old friend, Mamma?'

With a dismissive wave of her hand Mamma said. 'I must have mentioned her before, we know each other in Bishop's Stortford. Anyway, this is Maria. She has been studying in England and is now in Italy to continue her studies. She also needs work, I told Mrs. Watson that you would be able to give her a job. Maria has excellent typing skills and would make the perfect secretary for you.'

Maria was standing behind Mamma listening to all this and laughing. She looked at me and raised her eyebrows to let me know that she knew just what Mamma was up to.

'Allow me to find you a chair, Maria. I think you should be seated next to me, don't you?' I said picking up on Mamma's expectation and falling into the part. I took her hand and very gallantly kissed it. 'Mamma, you must sit next to Mr. Hampton here, you can keep him entertained, now that we have concluded our business. As I obviously have other interests to keep me busy this evening.'

Maria and I shared a look, full of conspiracy. And her smile answered my question perfectly. We both knew why we were there and to keep Mamma happy tonight, we would go along with it.

'So, do you have family here in Italy?'

'Some, on my mother's side. She's Italian, from Naples. But my Dad's English. I've been brought up with both languages. I studied to become a teacher and have a posting here as an English teacher.'

'So, you don't need a job? You are not continuing your

studies?'

Maria laughed and told me that Mamma was just using that as an excuse.

'Your Mamma does know my mother, they're not friends as such, but they use the same hairdresser. No more studying for me, it's time for me to teach. To impart my knowledge on all those children, as my Dad would say.'

'Of course, Mamma's been trying to find me a wife for so long now that I'm used to these legions of friends she has back in England. All with beautiful daughters, and I might add, she has excelled herself this time.'

Maria had the grace to blush. 'Your Mother didn't exaggerate when she told me of your good looks either. Or your charm. Your English is excellent by the way. I suppose being in the hospitality trade you need to know several languages?'

'Yes, I made a point of learning English and have passing German as well. I have to be able to talk to my customers.'

Mamma was quite busy telling George all about our family, I'm sure the poor man was totally bored by now. And he had the next day's flight to endure it all again, if she got her way. Which I don't doubt and be seated next to him.

Well I'd lost Fran again and Maria was really rather nice, to look at. She is intelligent, bright, amusing and yes very pretty. Her colouring is very Mediterranean, except for her eyes which are hazel. Not quite green, like Fran's and not blue. A quite pleasing colour. She has her hair cut in a short style which I must say suits her little oval face. Perhaps Mamma is right, and I should look to find a wife. Maybe, just maybe I could see how it goes with Maria, if she wants to that is.

'Would you like to come out to a quieter dinner with me one night this week, just us, not the rest of the family? Maybe tomorrow, after I've dropped Mamma off at the airport?'

'You know? I think I would'' She answered me. 'Will that make your Mamma happy; do you think?'

'Probably, but it would also make me happy.'

'Well then, let's do it.'

I looked at Mamma and saw a very satisfied smile playing at her mouth. Yes Mamma, you think you've at last got me settled. I'll go along with it, I thought, for now, and see where it takes us.

Poor George was being talked at by Mamma. I only hope he'd not put a lot of paperwork aside to catch up on while flying home.

I'd offered to give him a lift to the airport when I took Mamma and I think he now may have regrettied accepting that offer. I know that there was only a small chance that they would be seated together but I had the feeling that Mamma would somehow make that happen. I suspect he's never been faced with Italian Mothers before. Oh well, I'm sure he'll manage. So long as it doesn't put him off Italy for ever and decide to look for Spanish wines instead.

Chapter 13

Pieta

I'd not done this for a long while, take a lady out to dinner. I thought I'd take Maria to the old part of the town where there are some very nice restaurants that the locals eat in. Was I less likely to meet anyone I know there? I'm not sure why that should have bothered me except we wouldn't have a chance to be alone. If we met somebody that I knew they would have joined us. Usually this was fine but when you are trying to get to know someone it could be disruptive. It's not a part of the town I frequent much, as I'm usually based in the holiday sector.

'I'm entitled to take a beautiful woman out to dinner, and it shouldn't matter where we go,' I told Paulo.

Maria told me where her lodgings were and was to pick her up from there. I thought maybe I'd take a taxi so I could have a drink as well. Is that what the English call Dutch courage? Probably, but I felt like a teenager all wired up for a first date.

'Not tonight, the crisp white shirt, and black pressed trousers. You have a fine linen suit hanging in my cupboard that you should wear,' Guilia said. I was finding this both exciting and disconcerting and asked for her advice. It was the first time I'd entertained the thought of a woman permanently in my life. I'd had girlfriends but nothing serious. Fran, I had hoped would share it, my life, with me, this life I'd made for myself. But since then? Well it's been nothing but work.

When she came out of her lodging house, I saw a vision of beauty. Maria was wearing a fine silk dress and she looked gorgeous. How could any man resist? The cab took us to a nice restaurant, that I knew of and we found a small cosy booth to sit in.

'Your Mother went to England to be with your Father?'

'Yes, they met here while he was on holiday. Love at first sight, my Dad said. Mum, always laughs and says if that is so, how come she had to move to cold England to be with him? Why couldn't he move to Italy. He always said he would have but he can't stand the heat and says that they have their love to keep them warm.'

'And are they still in love?'

'Oh, very much so, but enough of this, tell me about your new business plan with poor Mr. Hampton. He'll have had a busy journey home with your Mamma.'

'I'm not so sure he wanted me to take him with Mamma to the airport this afternoon. I think he'd have preferred to go in a taxi, but Mamma insisted,' I laughed.

'Your Mamma has a way of getting what she wants. As do most Italian mothers.'

'Yes. Mamma can be quite formidable, but my father seemed to find a way round her.'

The rest of the evening we didn't talk much about Mamma and her plans to marry us off. But the conversation was flowing and very pleasant. We decided that we would like to see each other again and I asked her.

'Would you like to see my farm? I can take you there tomorrow. It's not just a vineyard, but I also have sheep, goats and cattle. Horses as well.'

'I would love to, it sounds glorious.'

'Well, I hope you like it, it is my pride and joy. Along with the hotel of course.'

Maria lifted her glass and we toasted.

'To, your pride and joy,' she said.

The evening finished with another taxi ride to her lodgings, and we ended the night with a quick peck on the cheek.
I got back to The Bacchus and walked into my office. Looked at Fran's picture and thought, maybe it's time. I took the painting from the wall and put it in the bottom drawer of my desk. A sadness crept over me but also, I was relieved to at last conclude that I've lost her. I never had her in the first place, did I?

I'm now thirty-three years old and I probably need to be thinking of having a family. Someone to leave all this too. Otherwise what's the point of it all.

'Hello Maria, I just wanted to make sure you are alright. Oh, and to say to bring a swim costume with you tomorrow.'

'Ha ha, of course I am alright, you just left me and now you call? Have some sleep Pieta and I will see you tomorrow and go to your farm complete with costume. Oh, and turn off your mobile. I don't want you calling any other ladies tonight.'

'Yes, I'll turn it off, just for you. Good night Maria.'
Was this how I should behave? I didn't know, I'd been out of the loop for so long, but I was quite excited at the prospect of seeing Maria again. She was such good company. I'm just wondering what she really thought of me, was that normal? We had similar work ethic, she's not let anything get in the way of her education and has achieved her goal. I have worked hard all my life and have more or less achieved mine.

When I took Maria to my farm the next day, I showed her around my house. It is a very old farmhouse which was in a dilapidated state when I bought it. Nearly falling down.

'For a couple of years while it was being restored to

how I wanted it I lived in a static caravan down by the barn.'

'How very brave of you,' Maria said. 'I think I could manage a caravan for a couple of weeks, but years?'

'It took a long time to restore the house because I was concentrating on the plans for the hotel and I was also making sure I had the farm up and running. So at least I had an income while I achieved my dream of the hotel.'

'And you have now achieved your dream. Wow, that is some kitchen.'

'When I'm here I like to cook for myself, so I had the kitchen laid out in the most efficient way, but I have everything I could ask for in a kitchen. My chef friend advised me of the essentials. Then I just bought everything I thought I would ever need to use.'

'So those drawers are full of every utensil or appliance ever invented?'

'Yes, more or less. Take a look.'

She opened a deep drawer and her eyes widened at the amount of stuff I had in there.

'Granite work tops to keep everything as cool as possible?' Running her hand gently along the surface.

'Yes, they're important for good food, I'm told.'

'Whatever is that, it's huge, is it your fridge?'

'It's the biggest I could get, had to fill that space somehow, didn't it?'

'Ha, ha there's enough space to hold food for a big family for a month. And is that a pantry I spy there? So much storage. Are you planning on catering for a big family then Pieta?'

'I like to be ready for any possibility,' I said smiling at her comments. 'Here's the utility room with a door to the yard. I can come in there and take all my dirty clothes off when I've been working on the farm.'

'I can't imagine you wearing dirty clothes, Pieta.'

'Ahh It's hard to keep clean sometimes.'

We went into the lounge area and Marie marvelled at the height of the ceiling.

'I made the lounge area double height which helps to keep it cooler in the summer. I told her. 'But I kept the open hearth with a wood burner to help take the chill off in the winter. That helps the underfloor heating just in case it turns very cold.'

'Oh, that's what's missing. Radiators. How clever.'

'Can I show you upstairs?'

'Oh yes, my mother will want all the details.'

'Upstairs I have four big bedrooms, each with an en-suite attached to it and the vistas from the windows are to die for.'

'Gosh, each room has its own beautiful view,' Maria, was enthralled.

'What a lovely home you have here.'

'Yes, that's why Mamma wants me to fill it with a wife and children.'

'Well, we'll have to see what we can do about that. Won't we? Just to keep your mother happy, you understand,' she said.

'It's always good practice to keep mothers happy,' I said smiling back at her. 'Outside the back of the house I've just finished the sun terrace which is big enough to hold a decent sized party, I hope. That's where the swimming pool is. The garden has just been set out, I'm no gardener, but when it grows the lawn will reach down to the stable block.'

'You did all this yourself?'

'Me and a few friends. It took us a while and I just did the labouring work. The technical stuff was down to my friend Roberto, who also built the stables. Very clever man is Roberto.'

'How many horses do you have here?'

'There's four, mostly out in the pastures, I can see them from my bedroom and if I ever have time to look out of my window, I love to watch them grazing. They're in at the moment because of the flies'

'How much time do you have to enjoy all this Pieta? As far as I can tell you are such a hard-working man that I wonder how you've achieved all this and it begs the question, why?'

I shrugged. 'It is what I always wanted. I have my dream now and I'll get to enjoy it soon. My big plan for my life has come about and I have as you say achieved what I set out to do,' I felt that this conversation was getting a bit too deep and personal. I liked this woman but didn't feel ready to share myself fully with her. Changing the subject, I asked,

'Do you ride Marie?'

'I love riding and used to go all the time when I was a child. I've not been able to keep it up lately though. I may be a bit rusty.'

We wandered down to the stables where my lad who does all the hard work with them, Daniel, saddled up a couple of the horses. Maria and I set off and I showed her around the whole farm. Riding round the vines and onto the cattle pastures, and sheep pastures.

'Forgive my ignorance but are these beef cattle or milk ones?'

'All beef cattle, the pasture is better for producing beef. But the sheep and my goats produce milk and I am thinking of starting a cheese production from them.'

'Is there no end to your talents?'

'Stop, you will give me a big head.'

I'd already planned what we should eat, I hoped she liked my cooking. But before dinner we went for a swim in my brand-new pool. She's the first person besides me to have a swim in there. It is perfectly round.

'How do you do lengths in this?' she said laughing. 'Or do we just swim around in ever decreasing circles?

'Yes, we could play chase round and round.'

'Just have to make sure you do as many circuits each way or you will end up lop sided,' Maria laughed.

We had a great day and I was beginning to see Maria would fit right in as the head matriarch of my household. I think.

Perhaps, I can fall in love with this woman. That would please Mamma and may be even please myself.

Mamma is back home now in England, undoubtably planning an autumn wedding. I hope she doesn't get carried away. It is early days for Maria and me. But I am beginning to think that now is the time for me to settle down and produce more than just money.

We managed a few days to be together, going out to lunch and seeing the sights. But now I'm needed at the hotel. We're getting busy there and with high season coming up it was all hands. Paulo's restaurant was doing really good trade. I'm so pleased that he found out that he's good at cooking and had another talent besides attracting young English girls. When he married my sister Bella, he turned his life around and became nearly as hard working as me. Now that seems to be paying off as he's thinking of opening another café. From our humble beginnings we now have the satisfaction of making a difference. Paulo of course has my sister and two lovely children to enjoy as well. I so far have no-one.

I'd not been open to any relationship and I think Mamma could be right that now was the time. I liked Maria, maybe love would grow?

Chapter 14

Fran

'You know that thing about six degrees of separation?' Dad said to me one Saturday morning. I'd gone around for a barbeque in their sunny garden. Sheila was bustling about fetching bowls of salad, marinated burgers and chicken pieces and thick cut vegetables to roast on the grill.

I'd walked to their house from mine which is only about two miles. Happy to do so because there was so much work for me to do and I had been sitting down all week. The work of a graphic designer does involve quite a lot of sitting and computer aided drawing. So, today I could allow myself a few glasses of wine as I don't have to worry about driving. Sheila's nephew was coming to stay tonight to celebrate starting his new job. He's moving into the area to take over as the new manager of a pet food company that was based in the town. Of course, I knew Charley pretty well, he's much the same age as me and we often meet up at family gatherings, usually at Christmas, weddings, funerals, the odd party, that sort of thing. We've always been friendly. He'd started at the pet firm as a Saturday boy, and had just kept on working there. He always said he preferred animals to people, but it was a kind of joke with him. He's a friendly, gregarious person and we've always got on well. I was looking forward to seeing him again.

'Yes, I've heard of it,' I answered smiling. Thinking I would have to remember to ask Jess the origin of the saying. I have the feeling it's from a novel.

'Well, I think you need to hear this. Sheila's mother's hairdresser. You know the one who visits her every fortnight to give her a wash and brush up. Well she has a rented chair in a salon in town. She works there three days a week and does her home customers on the other two.'

'Yes,' Sheila said as she brought out some bread rolls, she'd made earlier. 'She says that way she can keep up with all the changing trends of hairdressing. She can also get discount for her products. '

'She only does wash and blow dries for her home customers, though doesn't she?' I asked. 'All the complicated stuff she does at the salon. Perms and colourings?'

'Mainly, yes but she can do some route touch ups at home. And cutting, she can do that in the home as well.'

'Anyway, as I was saying, before I was so rudely interrupted.' Dad said. 'Fran needs to hear about the six degrees. So, first is Sheila, then her Mum. Next comes Jenny the hairdresser. Well, while she was in the salon a few days ago another customer was in who told her something she heard from a friend of hers. The friend she was discussing …..'

'Gossiping about, more like,' Sheila interrupted again.

'Okay, I concede that, gossiping. But the upshot is that the friend is none other than Mrs. Bianchi. Pieta's mother. I didn't realise she actually lived in England.'

'Yes, she was chatting to me on the plane before she found out who I was. She lives with her sister here, who had married an English man many years ago, and there both on their own now. Anyway, what about her? I think we have got to six now, haven't we? If you count the salon.'

'Well, the friend of Mrs. Bianchi was saying that her friend was going shopping for a very special outfit. She thought she would be needing it for the Autumn.'

'A Mother of the groom outfit, Fran,' Sheila said

quietly. 'For Pieta, who she is convinced is going to be married soon,' she added.

'Oh. I see.' It was a bitter blow, and just a confirmation that Pieta had never really loved me as he expressed in those letters. But why write them so eloquently expressing such love? When we met again, he had obviously got over that love. Perhaps that's why he was so cold at the farm and had walked off. But he wasn't cold, was he? He had held me and oh so gently brushed away my tears. Maybe seeing me made him realise that he didn't have the same feeling as I so obviously had? Or was it a case of changing as we get older? Would we have lasted in a relationship if we had actually got together? Or would we have drifted apart? If I thought I had successfully put Pieta back where he belonged, safely in the past I was very much mistaken. It would seem the that infinite times my heart could break was building up even more.

Putting the virtual steel rod up my back again, I smiled and said

'So, what time's Charley arriving?' I noticed Dad and Sheila steal a glance at each other. I wondered if they'd been expecting histrionics from me in my Mother's style. Oh, I will cry, but not here, not now. I am made of stronger stuff. Maybe Jess can come around later, if she isn't seeing George and we can have a good blub together.

'This time,' a voice rang out as Charley came through the gate brandishing a bottle of wine in each hand.

'Oh good, more wine stocks. Well done Charley. How are you my handsome nephew?' Sheila said, breaking the mood completely.

'Great thanks, Aunt Sheila,' he said kissing her with a flourish on the cheek. 'Uncle Frank, you're keeping well?'

'All good mate and quit with the Uncle; it makes me feel old.'

'Yes, you can stop with the Aunt as well,' Sheila said as she relieved him of the wine and took it indoors.

'Fran, hello Cuz. How are you keeping? I'm sorry to hear about the Ray thing old girl. Shame, I liked him,' he said as he leaned over to give me a big hug. 'But water under the bridge, hay?'

Oh, another saying to ask Jess about.

'I'm great, Charley, congratulations on the new job. When do you start? I suppose you'll be house hunting. To buy or rent?'

'I start in a couple of weeks and yes I'll be house hunting, renting to start with. I'm just looking to find some digs for a few weeks until I can get properly moved. The company will pay for me to stay in a hotel but that's so impersonal.'

'Wow, that's very generous of them. But I can understand that'd be a bit lonely and I don't suppose they'll run to a posh hotel?'

'No, more like bed and breakfast, I've had a quick peek online and there's some nice ones, so thought I'd come and give some of them a better look.'

'Well, you're staying here tonight at no charge. So, lets break open this wine.' Sheila commanded.

I thought I'd recognised the labels on the bottles and knew that it was Pieta's wine.

'Where did you come across this wine, Charley?'

'Oh, there is a super little shop in Ipswich. He wants to import wines from all over the continent and had just brought these ones back from Italy. Hampton's wines, it's called.'

'Well, that's such a coincidence, I know him. He's

Jess's new beau. And he'll quite likely be opening a distribution centre close to here if all these Italian wine deals go through. So, Jess tells me anyway. I love this stuff. We got quite a liking for it while we were there.'

I wondered if Charley had been invited round for this lunch as a consolation prize for me. But I put the thought to the back of my mind. That would have been more the sort of thing Mum would've done, and she would have invited Ray. A thought occurred to me and before I had much time to think it through, I heard myself saying it out loud.

'I have a spare room; you can stay in Charley. I've moved my office out of the house into the garden.'

'Oh, open plan? Or should I say open to the elements?'

'Oh, very funny. No, I've got rid of that old summer house and had a studio built out there. Much more professional for when I have clients around, and so much better than inviting them upstairs into a bedroom. I'm nearly finished and all up and ready for a grand opening inspection.'

'We can all pop round tomorrow and have a look,' Dad said. 'I'm dying to see the garden studio. And if you're sure about Charley staying with you for a while, he can take a peek at your spare room.'

'Yes, I'm serious, Charley you'd be welcome to my spare room until you get moved properly.' Feeling more positive about the decision.

'Well that would be great, much nicer than living in a hotel or a B&B. I can pay you my boarding allowance instead. Keep it in the family so to speak. Win, win, all round. Thanks Fran. Gosh I didn't think I'd be able to be comfortable while I got used to the new job. Let's drink to it shall we?'

'Have you seen Ray lately?' Dad asked.

'Oh, yes he keeps popping up, like the proverbial bad penny. The questions for Jess keep piling up. Where does that one come from? 'He still thinks he can come walking back and take up his life again. He's actually surprised that I am not falling around his feet in a dead faint, at the pleasurable thought of having him back. I'm convinced he's still getting encouragement from Mum. Despite Michael trying to hold her back.

'Well, if I move into your spare room for a few weeks do you think it'll make Ray back off?'

'It may help, he thinks I'm vulnerable on my own. And that I need a man to look after me. That's his mind set at the moment. How pathetic is that? After all he left me there to be alone, didn't he? '

'I'm sure he's just using that as an excuse to come around, he really should go and lay in the bed he made for himself. I know I shouldn't speak ill of your mother, but she really needs to sort her own life out,' Sheila ranted.

'Is business good then?' Charley said trying to defuse the situation a bit.

I smiled and said. 'Getting better all the time. And I can spend so much more time getting organised now. I get up, get dressed and go to work. Although the commute is only twenty meters down the garden.'

'Well, at least you're not at the mercy of public transport.'

'Er, no but it's handy because I still have some stuff in the bedroom, I haven't had time to move down and have to keep popping indoors to fetch. It's getting there slowly, bit by bit.'

'You'll get sorted out, love,' Dad said.

'Of course, I will. But it's as if I am at work and not

piffling about at home. There's even a separate phone line in the studio, and my computer's in there. I have a loo and a small kitchenette so once at work I can do my eight hours and then close the door and go home. That is, I might add, fantastic.' My enthusiasm for the project taking over my thoughts of Pieta.

'Sound's brilliant, darling. Good choice, so much better than renting office space in town. That would've been a bit expensive.'

'The only problem is I'm not doing any housework and my house is getting filthy. I could do with a lady that does. I always hated housework any way.'

'Sheila may know someone,' Dad said. 'How about our wonderful lady?'

'In fact, I think Irene's looking for more work. Yep for the price of a couple of good bottles of wine a week you could have a cleaner to do the housework.' Sheila piped in.

'And if I'm going to pay you my boarding allowance that's covered, for the time being any way,' Charley added.

'Today is getting better and better,' I said not feeling it at all.

'Talking of wine, this is nice, how much was it Charley?' Sheila asked.

'It's £12, at the moment but the chap is not sure what the price will be when they are getting it imported. He says he may be able to get it cheaper.'

'Is this your Pieta's wine then Fran?' Dad asked. 'It's a bit of alright.'

'Not my Pieta, by all accounts, but yeah he produced it on his vineyard, and now George is importing it.'

'George? Oh yes Jess' new fella.'

'I've got the job of designing the new labels, George

thinks that these ones won't stand out enough in the supermarkets. And he wants his own corporate image portrayed as well. So that he can get known as the importer of the finest wines.'

'Good business head he has then,' Dad commented.

'He's quite ambitious, and Jess likes him,' I said. Still wondering if I'd done the right thing inviting Charley to use my spare room.

Much later as I wandered home full of barbeque and a bit too much wine, I called Jess and told her of the news I'd heard about Pieta.

'Oh, really. Shall I come around tonight?'

'Yes please, I don't think I want to be alone right now. I'll think too much and cry too much.'

As Jess settled on my big fluffy settee she said. 'Maybe your Dad's six degrees of separation are just Chinese whispers.'

'Perhaps, or I really have lost him and any chance I had with him.'

'I honestly think that ship sailed some time ago. You can't go on living that particular dream. I'm sorry to sound brutal about it but it's time to let go.'

'True, I need that virtual steel rod up my back and to put a happy smile on my face. Get on with my life. Right now, I need to concentrate on building this business of mine, to get back some of the money I've spent on my new studio. Oh, come and have a look at the nearly finished article. There are still some bits of furniture upstairs that I, hate to admit, need strong men for.'

If I hadn't changed the subject, I would have dissolved into tears again. I really have lost him and steel rod or not I could recognise the emotion charging around my brain, the one that left me a quivering wreck of pain and sadness.

So, we went out and I showed Jess my creation.

'It's fantastic,' Jess enthused. Are you going to put a sign on the back gate, so people come in that way rather than through the house?'

'That's the plan, then I can lock up the house and go to work in the garden. Cool isn't it?'

'Oh, you have a message,' Jess pointing to the light flashing on the phone.

Pressing the play button, a voice I knew and loved, spoke to me. 'Hello, Pieta Bianchi, here. George Hampton gave me this number, so I thought I would just ring to say I am sending over an email with the wording for the new wine bottle labels. I hope that is alright and perhaps you will let me know if there is anything else you need. Thank you, Prego.'

I froze at the sound of his voice. Only a few minutes ago I was telling myself that I could live without this person and I had already moved on. My stomach knotted up and I felt tears spring into my eyes.

Jess pulled me outside and locked the door. She steered me into the house and made me sit down.

'It's still there isn't it?' she asked me.

I nodded, unable to say anything.

'I have to stop this, it's ridiculous, I can't carry on like this. All that's long gone, in the past. But it's so hard. Oh, how I wish we'd never gone to Rimini. We could have gone anywhere but I thought it'd be such a good idea to go there. How stupid was that? All this would have stayed up in Mum's loft in its little box,' I eventually managed to babble out.

'Life in boxes? Well that is one way to look at it. It's still very raw, we've only been home a couple of months and it was a shock to the system that when you met him again and remembered how much you felt for him. You know what they say? It's better to have loved and lost? That's Tennyson by the way. But I'm not sure about having loved twice and lost twice. And so soon after Ray as well. Seen him lately?'

'He keeps popping round. He wants to come back.'

'What? The cheeky bugger. After all he's put you through?'

'He thinks I'm lonely and vulnerable being here on my own. So why wouldn't I want a man here, to look after me? He's got the bit between his teeth and won't take no for an answer.' Looking at her questionably she picked up that I wanted an explanation of that saying.

'That's more or less self-explanatory when a horse decides to run away, he's said to clamp his teeth on the bit so there's no controlling him. Well, perhaps it's a good job Charley is moving in. For one thing it'll take thinking time away from you and give Ray something else to think about.'

'Charley will only be here for a few weeks until he finds a place of his own. I need to get his room sorted, I have loads of stuff up there that still needs to go in the studio.'

'There ya go. Something to focus on, while you shut Pieta into his little box, but for goodness sake don't forget to open your own box from time to time. You may well yet find someone who takes your mind off the Pieta box forever. I did, I found George,' Jess said.

'Yes, I must stop this, but I keep getting reminded, Dad's six degrees of separation seem to be getting closer all the time.'

'What's up in the spare room that needs bringing down?' Jess, trying to get me off the subject.

'Well, the main thing is that antique plan chest. You know the one that Dad bought me when I first started doing my own work? I have all the artwork for my first projects in there. I want to keep those but the chest itself'll be useful for ongoing work. I thought about putting it next to my desk so I can move the printer off there, give me a bit more space to spread out.'

'That big chest with a million drawers? That's massive.'

'It's not that big and only twelve drawers not a million. But it's bulky and a bit of a problem to get it moved.'

'I know the one, let's go and have a look.'
Upstairs we trooped, into my old studio. Now to be Charley's room. Feeling cheered by my lovely friend and her on going happy nature.

'Oh God, that is massive. We can't do that on our own. Even if we take the drawers out it would be too big for us to get it downstairs by ourselves. Wouldn't it?'

'I don't know, would it? It's not very heavy without the drawers. I suppose we could have a go, that's if you're up for it?'

'Want to give it a go? After we pop down for another slurp of wine that is? An alcohol boost is what is needed here.'

'Good plan,' and down we went to think about this. And finished that bottle off.

'Okay, let's go for it. We can do this, we're women that do, remember that,' Jess said determinedly.
Back upstairs we went the two of us. We took all the drawers out and stacked them in the corner of the room. Then we tried the weight of the chest. It's not heavy as I'd told Jess but a bit unwieldly for us, it's wide and hard to reach round. If we were each a few inches taller with longer arms it'd be easier. But we gave it a go, more pushing than lifting and after several false

starts we got it out of the room. The next step would be to get it to the stairs. Jess looked puffed out, for all her fitness. So, we went down to open the next bottle of wine.

'Lovely wine,' I said, 'but this isn't getting my chest down.'

'Time for another shifting session?'

This effort saw us manoeuvring it across the landing to the stairs. The top of the stairs, right in the way. Teetering over the edge.

'There's only one way to get more wine, and that's to get this thing down there out of our way,' Jess pointed out.

'I'll go down below and you steady if from the top. I told her.' Squeezing past to go down two steps. My mood had lightened and as I squished past the chest to take a couple of steps down, I said. 'Bye Jess, I'll see you later.' Carrying on walking down the stairs.

'Oi, get back here Frances Middleton!' she yelled and laughing I retraced my steps back up to her. We began the tricky manoeuvre of getting this unwieldy piece of furniture down the stairs.

It was like something out of a Laurel and Hardy movie or the Chuckle brothers. In fact, we started giggling and saying, to me, to you. We managed to get it down without damaging too much of the plaster on the staircase wall. It needs decorating anyway, I can do that, after all I'm a woman that does. But when we got it to the hallway. Well, it was time to stop for another drink.

'I don't think I've laughed like that for years,' I said collapsing on to the settee.

Jess could hardly contain herself enough to pour more wine for us. And there I'm afraid the chest stayed. In the hallway, in the way. While we consumed the rest of the wine and giggled the night away. All night. Jess didn't go home.

'Oh, Jess, I really needed that. I said Sunday morning as I was putting the kettle on to make coffee.

'Laughter is the best medicine. That one comes from Proverbs by the way. Now all we have to do is get it out and down the garden.'

'I think we'll have to go out the front door and round the house to the gate. I suspect the way out to the back is a bit narrow, the gap'll be too small and it's a tight turn to the door.'

'Oh, that will give the neighbours a laugh.'

'Well we can have this coffee and think about it for a while.' Shall we sit out in the back garden? I need to sort that out as well. Ray always used to do the garden, he liked to keep it tidy. Right now, it is a wild garden and broken by all the building work.'

'There you go, something else to keep you busy, learning about gardens and how to look after them.'

'Ha ha, I just need to know which are weeds and which are plants.' I have some books somewhere that Ray left behind. Better study them.'

'Oh, weeds are flowers too, once you get to know them, as Winnie the Poo, says. Just one thing, why are you boiling the kettle for coffee?' Jess asked pointing to the hugely expensive coffee machine that Ray had installed when we remodelled the kitchen.

'Do you know what? I haven't used that since the day Ray walked out. There are loads of capsules in the cupboard.'
So not only did we have a laugh, but this morning's hangover was sorted out with a proper cup of coffee.

Chapter 15
Pieta

When I phoned the graphic design office in England and left my message, I knew at once that George had commissioned Fran to do my labels.

'Hello, unfortunately Middleton designs are closed at present but do feel free to leave a message and I'll be in touch. Oh, your name and phone number would be helpful. And-um-oh-yes, after the beep. Many thanks.'

It was definitely her voice. So, she's started her own business. Well good for her, I wonder if her husband helps with that. I'll have to ask George when he comes out again. Not that I should be interested, she is a married lady and I now have Maria. When Fran was here that one time, I got to hold her, it felt so good. When she cried. I wanted to stop the tears, to make everything better and keep her with me forever.

Married lady or not I was very tempted to kiss her lovely mouth and make love to her. I had the feeling she would have wanted it as well. But I had to walk away before I lost all control. I'm beginning to wish that she'd not come here, I'd been able to put her out of my mind and have achieved so much. I loved that English girl, and I now know I still love the English woman as Mamma calls her, rather spitefully. Is that fair on Maria? No.

Could I build a good relationship with Maria now? I had to try and hope I could put my heart into it. But hearing Fran's lovely voice, even in a message? Well it set me back a couple of steps, for sure. I'd sent the email and the wording for the labels, all correct, it had been checked many times. There was to be four different wines going to England, Red, rose, a still white and a sparkling white. All must have a description, the blend, the alcohol level and energy levels printed on the back. Much the same as the labels sold in Italy. I could see Mamma, being proud to show off my wine to all her friends. Graciously, giving a bottle for the tombola, and preening when someone won it. All her friends would have bottles for their birthday and Christmas presents.

As for her "mother of the groom" outfit. I hoped she wasn't thinking of autumn of that year. Perhaps I should have told her to buy one for each season. I had hardly had a moment to see Maria. With it being high season and I was tied up in the hotel and making sure everything ran to plan for my guests. Soon it would be grape harvest time which was even more important to get right. Then Maria would be starting at her job in the academy. I know she'd been working hard to prepare for that and was very nervous. I don't want a wife who felt she must stay at home, I wanted her to be fulfilled and have her own career, if that is what she wanted. I felt under pressure to try and make this work, to see as much of Maria as I could but knowing it's what everyone wanted made it unreal, not quite wholesome.

'Why don't you just take some time off to be with her? You have good staff that are well trained. You're not indispensable.' Paulo is often saying to me. 'Bella will help out as well, she prefers the hotel to the restaurant. I think I work her too hard.'

'I don't want to leave the hotel right now. It's the first year and what if I'm needed for something?' Is that another excuse or a real reason?

'You're obsessive about it and even the boss of Best Western or Hilton takes a holiday every now and again.'

'Guilia and Ricardo are both being of great help. But in its first year of my hotel being open after planning and building for so long, I didn't want to leave it. And with the prospect of my wines travelling to England also a very important year for the vineyard. Strange how it all came together at the same time after all these years of hard work.'

'You have been obsessed with building the business, my friend, you can be quite boring at times,' Paulo said

I could make more time for Maria, but she understood how important this all was for me. I also needed to give her space, after all she was about to start her first job and had much to think about. In so many ways she reminded me of Fran. The independent nature of them both, how they were both determined to have a career outside the home. Some of the girls I've known have looked upon being a wife and mother as their career. That makes for a very happy marriage, I know.

'Bella and Guilia both go to work and look after the children, but they don't look upon their work as careers but as side-lines to their marriage. Their jobs earn them the money to treat themselves to shopping trips. Both are very happy and there's nothing wrong with that as far as I can see, but I think it is important for a wife of mine to have something outside the home.' I explained to Paulo.

So, soon I would be able to make more time for Maria and myself. Soon. When I'd have run out of excuses.

'That's just it though isn't it Pieta?' Bella asked me. 'What can be more important than your happiness and your future?'

'Oh, Bella, I just need to get all this sorted out then I will have more time.'

'You've spent the last fifteen years getting things sorted. Have you not given yourself enough time?

Maria would make you a good wife. She will work with you and make a family man of you at last. Don't leave it too late. She won't wait forever, and neither should she.'

'Soon, Soon. I'll be able to take time off and spend it with Maria. Not just right now, everything is just about coming together after all the preparation. I need to see this year through.'

Maria and I managed to get together about one night a week. I'd pick her up from her lodgings and we went to dinner. Each time I saw her I explained why I had not got more time. She told me she understood and was happy that we were not living in each other's pockets. We'd chat and laugh about inconsequential things. We had good times when together and although it was slow progress, we are finding a lot of similarities that we liked about each other. I'd then take her back to her lodgings and hand her over to the care of the formidable Signora Rossi. And would kiss. Yes, Maria understood, I know she did. She wasn't pushing for more.

Chapter 16
Fran

Jess and I finished our third cup of coffee and thought it was about time to get the chest out of the house into the studio. So, again we giggled our way through the task. Of course, we had to manhandle, or should I have said woman handle, it through the front door and out onto the driveway. So far so good, the door jam's still in one piece. But now we had to get it round the house and across the muddy ruts in the garden to the studio. Where are the Mr. Shifter and Co., when you need them?

'I Know!' I yelled when a flash of inspiration hit me. 'Derek has a sack barrow.'

'A what?'

'I'll show you,' and hot footed it round to next door. Knocking on the door of the neighbouring house I waited patiently for Derek to answer.

'Do you want me to come over and help with that?' he asked as he opened the door. Sack barrow in hand already. How did he know what I wanted?

Jean popped her head around Derek and told me they'd been having a good old chortle about our antics to get the chest out of the house.

I laughed and said I was glad to be a source of Sunday morning entertainment.

Jean looked me right in the eye and said. 'It's good to see you laugh again, my dear. You've been sad for far too long.'

'Thanks, I said feeling as if I wanted to cry in her shoulder but hiding it with a cheery smile. 'Oh, by the way, my cousin is going to be staying with me for a few weeks, so, if you see a strange man coming and going it will be him.'

'Oh, not a new lover then,' Derek said with a cheeky smile. 'I was going to offer myself for that position.'

'Really? And what does Jean have to say about that?' Jean laughed and said, 'You can have him, and his snoring. I'm surprised he doesn't wake you up with it.' And her laughter echoed across the street.

I do love my neighbours, I thought as I wheeled the sack barrow back to my driveway where Jess was waiting.

'Well, there you are. No shortage of potential lovers around here is there?'

'Right if I lift this end up and you pop the lip of the barrow under that we can tip it up and wheel it round to the studio.' I told her, ignoring her comment, which was loud enough for Derek and Jean to hear. And their laughter as they closed their door could also be heard far and wide.

Eventually after lots of pushing and pulling we got the chest to the door of the studio. I don't think I have had so much fun for a long time. Things had been so confusing and sad lately. But my mood was brightened and for the first time since Ray upped and left, I felt like me. The happy, cheerful person I used to be.

'Time for more coffee', Jess said. 'Then we'll go about getting it in and positioned where you want it.'

'Did I hear the magic word coffee?' said a voice. Charley had wandered through the open gate and watched us struggling with the chest.

'How long have you been standing there?' I demanded of him. 'You could have helped.'

'I still can as I am so much taller than either of you.' He smiled. 'But coffee first?'

'Yes, more coffee,' Jess piped up.

'Be round in a minute,' called another voice. Derek

from over the fence in his back garden. 'That's if you're making proper coffee, none of that instant stuff'.

'Well it looks as if we are having a party. Is Jean coming?' I called.

'Oh, that sounds lovely. I'll be right over as well'. And that's how our Sunday morning went. Jean came around and made the coffee and she brought croissants, for our breakfast. Derek, Charley and John, my neighbour from the other side all got the chest into my studio. I set my printer on it and fixed the wires, so they didn't show to my desk where the computer was sitting. Charley went up to have a look at his room and between the three men the drawers for the chest were bought down and put back in place. Complete with my artwork.

'Well, your room's now clear of all my studio stuff and you can arrange it however you like. As I've got the en-suite, the bathroom is yours to use. When are Dad and Sheila coming over?'

'Oh, they said they'd pop in this afternoon but if it isn't convenient to give them a ring.'

'This afternoon is fine,' I said. Knowing Mum was going out with Michael so wasn't likely to come round. Although Mum and Dad were getting on much better now, it's still advisable not to have them all in the same place at once. Especially not my house.

I had wondered why I started this whole studio project whilst it was going on. It all seemed such a hassle, but now it was finished I'd decided that it was worth all the expense. As well as all the negotiating with planners and building control. It left me with no savings now, but I did still have an income from my shares in Ray's business. And my own business was picking up nicely. And Charley coming along with his boarding allowance was also very fortuitous.

Chapter 17
Fran

Charley moved into his room a few days later. At least the neighbours had met him and knew who he was, so there shouldn't be too much curtain twitching going on in the road. He still had a few days before he started his new job. I set him to work on tidying and repairing my garden. After all, there was little point in having such a fantastic studio to make my business look more professional, if people had to use a machete to cut through the jungle to get to it. Ray had been the gardener and he had laid it out very nicely with seating areas in all the sun traps. But I'd neglected it and with it now being at the height of summer it was overtaking my poor efforts to keep it down. Also, some bits had been ruined by the building works.

I set about painting the garden gate so that it looked nice and tidy and put up the sign I'd made. I also made some tasteful little arrows pointing the way to the back of the house. My large front driveway could easily accommodate three cars, so mine, Charley's and one for customers. Or of course Jess. Also, I've been up to quite a few things lately that are not normally in my remit. I changed my old banger for a more modern car, one that befits a single lady. Not the most practical but a cute little sports car. I've been with Jess to the sunbed centre, as I'd picked up a bit of colour while we were in Rimini, and I thought maybe I could keep it up. Jess took me to her nail salon, as she said, and I agreed that it looked better to have proper nails and not ragged bitten stumps when presenting myself to customers.

But all this cost money and I was now getting rather short of that commodity. So instead of joining the gym that Jess goes to I've taken up running. That doesn't cost me anything, well not too much anyway after buying the expensive trainers Jess insisted on. I've also employed a lady to come and clean the house three times a week, the lovely Irene. So, at least the hated housework is taken care of. She'll even do my ironing and told me the other day that for an extra £5 from Charley she'd do his as well. Fantastic, all sorted. Ironing is one of the most hateful jobs to do in the house as far as I'm concerned.

When Ray and I were together he was pretty good at keeping the house clean. His tolerance levels of muck and tidiness were much lower than mine. While I would look at a job and think I would get on with that at some point, he would just do it. I missed that. But I couldn't let him anywhere near the washing and ironing. He ruined so many clothes. One time he had no uncrumpled shirts to wear and instead of getting on and ironing them I popped out and bought him some new ones. I had such a mountain sometimes, that I would nip down the local shop and buy a DVD to watch while ironing. Standing there pondering on a Tom Hanks one or something with Bradley Cooper in it one day a lady who I vaguely knew came over.

'Ironing?' she asked.

I laughed, 'How did you guess?'

'Me too,' she said brandishing a copy of something romantic. 'Take the Tom Hanks, you don't want to be ironing your fingers, watching Bradley Cooper.'

'Good point,' I said and took the Tom Hanks. Well at least the mountain became a hill that day and over time I collected quite an impressive collection of DVDs. And now I have the wonderful Irene who will do it all.

Chapter 18.
Pieta

Mamma informed me that she'd be coming for another little holiday. With it being September and she expected the hotel to be slowing down, I was sorry but also satisfied to have to tell her that the hotel was still fully booked all the way through to the end of October. But things were running quite smoothly now, and I'd taken time away from there to help with the grape harvest and watch the wine being started on its production. She would stay with me at the farm. I have to say she was a bit put out at not being able to stay in the centre of town, but I could hire a car for her. She's not the best driver in the world. That was always a worry. Not only here in Italy however, I suspect she was even worse in England, but at least, she could go visiting all her friends and be on hand to visit Guilia and Bella.

'I can drive her about and so can Bella,' Guilia said.

'She will be happier if she has her own transport. Something small, but stylish,' Bella told me.

'She can pop in and grace the hotel with her presence as well as Paulo's restaurant and café. I'm not sure how long she's staying but she did mention that she needs to renew her gym membership before the end of the month. But she won't be short of opportunities to do her exercise in the hotel gym and swim in the pool,' I said. Mamma liked to keep trim and loved it when people compared her to the rather delicious Sophia Lauren. I know that being her son made me biased but still considered my Mamma as beautiful.

I'd be picking her up from the airport and Maria' came with me. We are both a bit nervous about that. Maria was quiet the other night when we were having dinner.

There was something on her mind and I could see she wasn't looking forward to what she was going to say. After forcing the conversation for some time, I eventually asked.

'What is it my love, what is bothering you so, tonight?'
She smiled at me with a sad comforting smile and said.
'That's just it, the "My Love" bit, we don't do we? Love each other that is.'

I was quiet as I knew exactly what she meant. We've become good friends and had a rather platonic love but as for romance, and attraction, we'd never got past the first kiss. Even that, whenever was more the kiss of siblings. No passion or fire. I nodded, and she went on.

'I've been offered a job back in England. Teaching Italian in an English school.'

'You've been headhunted? Or have you been searching for jobs in England?'

'Not head hunted, no. But I have been looking and it's a job I had already turned down. To come here. They wrote and offered me more money. I've decided to take it.'

'You are so unhappy here in Italy? You haven't even started the job here yet?'

'Not unhappy, Pieta, but not satisfied and I find I do miss being so far from my parents.'

'I understand. When do you start the new job?'

'Not till the end of the month. The school is a private one and their term starts later than most schools. They like to settle the children in to school life before they begin lessons as well. So, I still have just over a week before I must go.'

Did the bottom drop out of my world? No, it didn't. Oh, don't get me wrong, I was a bit disappointed but not devastated that Maria was leaving. But I also felt the pressure leaving me. I'd been saved from this performance, this forced relationship with all its expectations. I could tell that Maria felt the same.

So we were at the airport and both nervous at telling Mamma that her scheme to get me married off and to continue her dynasty has failed.

'PIETA!' The voice reached us in its operatic tone long before Mamma did. The whole arrivals hall heard her. 'MARIA!' her fine tone came again. 'Oh, my two little love birds how lovely to see you both.' Mamma gushed as loud as she could and rushed to us with open arms crushing us both in an embrace to rival any dramatic performance. Mamma is home, I thought.
Before we even left the airport, she asked. 'So how much longer are you going to make we wait?'

'For what, Mamma?' I asked innocently.

'The announcement. When am I going to have my long-awaited daughter-in-law? How much longer do you two need, before you set a wedding date?'
Maria shrunk at least an inch trying to hide her embarrassment.

'We'll discuss this later, shall we? Not here?' I suggested.
Picking up her cases I steered her out of the arrival's hall towards the car park. As the door closed, I was sure I heard a round of applause break out inside.

'How am I to have more grandchildren before I get too old?'

'Mamma, you already have five, how many more do you want?'

'But none from you,' She said emphatically. 'Just what is the hold up?'

'When we get home, we'll explain to you everything, but not here.'

Thank goodness on arriving at the farm Guilia and her children were there, making it impossible to have our discussion.

Maria said she would come around to the hotel where I was planning on taking Mamma to dine that night and we would explain it all to her there. Maybe if she was in public she wouldn't be to theatrically upset. Maria had the mark of Mamma.

While we were seated at dinner, we told Mamma how it was between us and that Maria was going back to England the following week. To give her dues Mamma was quiet and took it all in.

'So, my task begins all again?' another of her dramatic sighs. 'I must trawl through my friends once more to find a wife for you. Oh, Maria I thought I had selected the right one with you. I thought you two would make the perfect couple and give me such pretty grandchildren.'

Maria could hardly hold back the tears of laughter. She assured Mamma that we had tried, and it just didn't work. She told Mamma of her new job and that she missed her parents and would just really rather live in England.

'I see, my dear. I see. I will go back next week as well, perhaps we will be on the same flight?'

'I may well come over also,' I said. 'I've been invited to view the new distribution centre George is setting up. He told me that he already had the building for it, and it wasn't being used to its best advantage at that time. He decided that the place, being so close to the motorway was better used as the main centre. It'd be ready to accept my wines and the others he had contracted very soon.'

I was telling all this to Mamma to take her mind off her

failed attempt to marry me off.

'Will we all travel together? Oh, that will be fun, not to have to talk to strangers on the way home,' She said

'Since when have you had difficulty talking to anyone? Strange or otherwise?'

'Oh, bad boy.' She hit me rather harder than that comment warranted. 'But George was such good company last time, he told me all about the wines and how he is going to be the sole distributor and how your labels are going to change for the English Market. Yes, we chatted quite a lot. But not all about wine.'

'Oh, what are you trying to get him married off as well?'

'No need, he is smitten. With the English Woman's friend. They at least are going to have a wedding.' she said sighing dramatically. 'Oh, by the way, talking of the English Woman.'

'Yes?' My heart doing a triple salko inside my chest. 'What of her?'

'I know people who know her, I have many friends in England. As you well know.'

'And?'

'Oh, you will never guess. I heard it in the salon while I was having my hair done, I can't be letting the grey show too much, I'm not old enough to be looking like a grandmother.'

'Of course, you're not,' Maria said.

'Your hair looks lovely as always,' I managed to say politely just wishing she would get on with her story.

'Yes, one of the other girls in the salon, she does home hairdressing, you know for those poor old dears who can't get out much. '

'Yes?' again I prompted.

'Well she goes to one of the care homes near me.'

Taking a drink, she asked. 'Is this one of the wines you are sending to England?'

'Indeed, it is,' I said smiling to hide my frustration, but Mamma always takes her time telling a story. It'll come out eventually, you just have to wait.

'It should do very well, for the English taste. Perhaps a bit too nice, but if George sells it for the right price and he picks up the more discerning customer I think it'll be alright.'

'Well, thank you Mamma.'

'Well, you know that I know my wines, I've always had impeccable taste,' she said but I've never seen her drink much of it and then only mine.

'The hairdresser?'

'Oh, yes. Well, one of the old ladies in that home is the grandmother of your woman. Or at least she is the mother of the person her father is married to. A bit complicated but that's the English for you.'

'Her parents are not together?' They were when here on their first holiday.'

'Hmm, divorced soon after apparently. And he married again, and it is HER mother who my hairdresser friend knows.'

'So' Fran's parents are divorced?'

'Yes, Pieta, please try and keep up.'
Holding up my hands in surrender I said. 'I'm with you now.' I looked at Maria and she was smirking and trying to hide her amusement.

'Well, she isn't married. Not anymore, she is divorced as well. What a family! Can they not keep a marriage together? What ever happened to "till death do us part"?' My poor husband died, and I have been a widow for so long. But they seem to swap and change all the time, no bother.'

115

'Fran?' The triple salko churned in my chest.

'Yes, Fran, what a name as well, why can't the use proper names? What sort of name is that?'

'Well Isabella is shortened to Bella,' Maria said reasonably.

'She is Frances,' I said. 'But I like Fran, it's a nice name and it suits her.'

'You would like such an English name. Anyway, the husband was unfaithful, and she kicked him out. Well how stupid is that, all men are unfaithful. But to give up so easily? No staying power, these English Women.' Maria looked at me questionably. I know she was thinking that Mamma was referring to her own marriage. And it was true that Papa was not monogamous. Poor Mamma. But that's all in the past.

'So, this has happened since they were here?'

'No, no, no, long before. The husband has a son with someone else. Probably why he went. If she couldn't or wouldn't give him children.'

'So, when she was here in May and you wouldn't give me any chance to talk to her,' I said looking Mamma directly in the eye so that she knew how I felt. 'She was a divorced woman then?'

Mamma shrugged. 'I suppose so. Anyway, take me home I need my beauty sleep. Will I see you tomorrow Maria?'

'Not tomorrow, I have many things to sort out,' She said smiling. She stroked my arm as she left and gave me a peck on each cheek. Yes, Maria understood what all this meant to me.

'We'll talk,' She said.

I nodded as I guided Mamma out to the car. I was angry with her for interfering, but I had to keep it in check. How was she to know that I still had such deep feelings for Fran? That I think it was because of those feeling that I couldn't get closer to Maria? What a waste of all our time. I don't know what Fran's feelings are toward me, but I could have found out back in May. But now I could. I'd go over on the same flight that Mamma and Marie are taking and go and see her. She was after all, doing my labels, so I had a legitimate right to see how they're looking.

Mamma would get over her disappointment and Maria would be happy again. How was I to be greeted by Fran? I wanted to know about my letters and if she ever received them? If Mamma hadn't taken so badly to her back in May then I could have found out about her divorce. How differently would I have been able to behave towards her? I could have told her then of my undying love for her. Maybe she'd have rejected me, even laughed, but at least I would have known. I didn't feel sorry about Maria, we gave it our best shot. But she sensed that my heart wasn't in it and she protected hers from me as well. Maybe that was lucky. Bearing in mind the news I've just had.

George told me I could give my consent or not to the wine labels online through email, or go and see the designer. Why had he chosen Fran to do the designs? Is her friend Jess trying to manoeuvre us here? Much subtler than Mamma's efforts I have to say.
At home and Mamma tucked up in her bed I got my laptop fired up and booked myself on the flight the following week to accompany Mamma and Maria back to England. I hadn't had a holiday for fifteen years, and this one would be a working one, so I think I deserved some time to myself. Guilia and Bella would be surprised.   I would speak with George and arrange everything. And I could see Fran, find out if there was

any hope for me there. I may have been setting myself up for a massive fail, but I had to know.

Chapter 19

Fran

In the time that Charley had been living here I'd been much more focused on my work. I'd gone to my office each day and worked hard to finish off all my outstanding projects and been able to concentrate on the Labels. George gave me a range of colours he'd like used and I have found a picture of Pieta's farm that I took when we first arrived there in our coach.

'I could make use of that. It's a great photo, even if I do say so myself,' I told Dad, on the phone one day.

'Well, I'm glad it's working out for you, my love,' he said.

'It turns out that Charley is an amazing cook, and he takes over the kitchen every other day. We've had some real gourmet style meals. Unfortunately for him when it is my turn we often have take-away or leftovers.'

I was never a domestic goddess. I could rustle up simple dishes but usually it was a case of sticking my head into the freezer at about five and having it ready on the table by the time Ray came home at six. I did like doing dinner parties but would take all day about it. We've settled into a pattern, Charley and me, which began much earlier in the day than I was used to. We'd go running very early. His idea is to get it over with, he said. Whereas I'd have left it till later, but it was a good way to start the day, then get showered and go to work. I could almost keep up with him, so I must have been getting fitter. It was pleasant having him in the house and he was easy company. I didn't notice how lonely I'd been here, alone in this house. And he kept Ray at bay. 'Well, I'm not alone here, now am I?'
Except that one time. It was Ray's first visit since

Charley had moved in. He knew of course because Mum must have told him. He always suspected Charley of fancying me but then again Ray would have accused the clouds of flirting if I stared at them too long.

I was in the kitchen with arms full of vegetables to chop up and roast when Ray walked in. He just grabbed me and kissed me. I was so surprised that I dropped all the vegetables all over the kitchen floor and pushed him away.

'What are you doing?' I squeaked in shock.

'Oh, come on Fran, you know I really want to be back with you. I know we could make a go of it if we both put in some effort. We were good together, and with both of us trying we could be again.'

I backed off and started to try to reason with him but then lost all sense of proportion. I was seething with anger and through gritted teeth I told him.

'Ray, we were never that good together, and if I remember rightly it wasn't me who didn't put in the effort. It was all a bit one sided.'

Then really getting annoyed with him standing there looking so sure of himself. 'You were the one who took our marriage vows so lightly.'

Charley walked in at this point.

'Hello Ray, alright mate? How's it going?'

'So, it's right, what I've been hearing. This common gossip that's doing the rounds, you've moved in.' Turning to me he accused. 'Didn't take you long to replace me did it. And your cousin for God's sake?'

'Excuse me?' What do you mean, common gossip? And you weren't sluggish replacing me, either were you?' I asked shocked at his attitude.

'Hang on a minute there, Ray, I'm just lodging here for a few weeks.'

'Hah. Lodging? Yeah Right! Getting your feet under my table with my wife in my house.'

'WOW wait a minute!' I screeched at him. 'It's not your house, and I am not, repeat not your wife. And that there, is not your table. I'm perfectly at liberty to have whoever I want to lodge here.' I was fuming and all the resentment at his behaviour boiled over and filled the kitchen with hate and vile anger.
Charley tried the reasonable approach. 'I think it's time you went home isn't it Ray? To your wife and son?'

'What has it to do with you?' After all you are just the lodger? So, you tell me.'
Charley went to him and put his hand on Rays shoulder. 'Come on mate, time to leave.'

'Get your hands off me, and in future keep them off my wife.'

'I've never even met your wife. Sam is her name isn't it?'
Just at he said it the very person walked in the back door carrying Dylan. Her tears already falling.

'I knew you'd be here; I saw your car in the driveway.' Ray was silenced by her appearance. He had the grace to look ashamed of his behaviour. Which, I have to say was not typical. I felt so sorry for this girl that I had for so many months hated with all my heart. But she just looked broken standing in my kitchen.

'Sam,' Ray began.

'No, Ray. Please don't say anything more. Don't try telling any more lies. I've had enough of them. All the lies and the missed dates. All the times I've longed for you to come home and cried all evening waiting for you. I'll be moving out as soon as I can. You obviously don't want me and Dylan. Please don't come home tonight.' She turned and ran out.

I followed her; I couldn't leave her to cope with this alone. She had the baby to think of as well. I caught up with her before she could drive away because she was settling Dylan into his car seat.

'Sam, are you going to be alright? '

One look at her face told me what I needed to know. Of course, she wasn't. All the hate I felt for her melted away and was replaced by more fury at Ray. He had treated both of us badly.

'I didn't encourage him you know. I've sent him home from here often,' I told her.

'No? You here on your own? You couldn't give us a clean break, could you. You couldn't leave us to the business. Sell your shares to Ray like he asked and just let us get along. You had to keep a hold on him didn't you.'

I was having a problem understanding just what she was saying. Had Ray been using that as an excuse to come around here? He really told her that?

'What? Whoa, wait a minute. He's never asked me to sell him my shares. He even said it'd be better all-round if I just took a dividend. He said he couldn't afford to pay me out anyway.'

The penny dropped then and I saw the resignation cross her face. 'So, he wasn't coming here to try to persuade you to let go of the company?'

'No, I would happily let go but he didn't want me to.'

'But he said.' She couldn't finish the sentence.

She hugged Dylan closer to her and broke down, crying so hard. I put my arms around her and the baby. I'd not seen such sadness bubbling out of someone for many a long year. Her heart was well and truly broken. I couldn't let her go, not like that. I guided her to the front door and led her into the lounge and got her to sit down.

'Wait there for a minute,' I said to her.

Back in the kitchen Charley was picking up the dropped vegetables and Ray was leaning against the work top, his arms folded and seething with barely restrained temper.

I opened the back door, looked directly at him 'GET OUT NOW,' I yelled rather loudly. 'And don't ever come here uninvited again, do you hear me? Oh, and I'm having a valuation done on your, on our company. Then you WILL take a loan to pay me out. I'll not ever have to have anything to do with you again. 'GET OUT!' As I was yelling this tirade at him, I advanced on Ray, shaking with anger.

To do him justice he went out of the door and walked around the house without a backward glance. I took a few calming breaths, that yoga can come in handy sometimes.

I went through to the lounge to see Sam standing at the window watching him go. I put my arm round her shoulder. And she leaned back into me. Then I don't know what possessed me, but I heard the words coming out of my mouth before I could stop them. What is it about my runaway mouth at the moment?

'You and Dylan can stay here if you like until you can get something else sorted.'

She turned to me and said. 'Really? That would be wonderful. Mum will have to do some shuffling about to accommodate the two of us. It will only be for a few days, honestly. But I would be so grateful. Why are you being so nice? Especially to me. The one who stole your husband?'

'Door mat, me. Anyway, if Ray had really respected me, he would never have gone off with you. But at least you have him,' I said indicating Dylan who by this time had fallen asleep out of pure emotional exhaustion, I'm sure. Poor little mite.

'I need to feed him,' Sam said as Charley walked in with three cups of tea. She was still in a bit of a dither. 'I don't know what to do,' She wailed.

'Have a cup of tea, it's the cure all for shock. The baby's fine. He's asleep, and you need this before you wake him up to feed him,' he stated reasonably. 'Right, takeaway it is tonight then, What? Indian, Chinese, or Pizza? On me.'

I thought I'd better introduce Charley and Sam, as they had never met.

'Well as I am no longer breast feeding can I have a Chinese?' Sam asked. 'Do you think Ray's really gone? I need to go to my car and get Dylan's bag.'

'I'll get it for you,' Charley said heading out of the front door.

'Can I really stay here Fran? Are you sure? I don't want to be in the way. I can always go home. I don't suppose Ray will be there anyway. I'm not sure where he goes but he'll stay away for a few days. He does that sometimes. I thought he was here, with you.'

'No, not here. I wouldn't have him. And yes, it's fine you can stay here till your Mum can fit you in.'

We ate our Chinese in the kitchen at the table that Ray thought Charley was getting too close to. In the kitchen I might add that was expertly cleaned by my lodger. Then I took Sam upstairs. To the third bedroom. The smallest one, not really big enough for two.

'It's only a little room but should do you for a couple of days.'

'It's great and thank you.'

I left her there with Dylan as she had to phone her mum

and tell her all that had gone on. Halfway down the stairs I thought, whatever have I let myself in for? How will Ray take this? I still couldn't believe his behaviour today. Not like him at all. I really couldn't understand what had got into him.

My phone rang. 'Hello Mum.'
She said. 'Are you okay? Ray's just been here and told me he had been really stupid. He has gone now but he worried me. Has he been round to you?'

'Yes, he has, and caused a bit of an argument to say the least.'

'Well I definitely didn't put him up to that. So, don't go blaming me this time.'

'It's alright mum, Ray's big enough and stupid enough to cause his own ructions without any help from you or me.' I told her what had happened.

'Oh God, I suppose it is down to me then. I told him Charley was moving in, but only to stop him going on about you being alone in the house and vulnerable.'
I laughed. 'Don't worry about it, Mum but if you want to meet your grandson in law you had better pop over as Sam's staying here for a few days.'

'Oh, how lovely, will she mind do you think?'

'I shouldn't think so. See you tomorrow then? Bye Mum.'

'Bye darling.'

We made a plan between us that evening, that on the following Monday when Ray should be at work Charley and Sam would go to the house and clear her stuff out. She would store, in my garage, what she didn't need directly, and then as soon as her mother had a room sorted, she would move everything there. It's amazing how much stuff you needed for such a small baby. However, did I think I could fit children in this house?

Rosemary, Sam's mum, came here to sit with me and look after Dylan while Sam and Charley were out. I was somewhat nervous about that but then again maybe she is as well, I thought. But she's really nice. And I must say, I've not noticed Charley being quite so chivalrous before.
So, for a while my house will be full, really full. More than ever it has been before.

One day I heard Sam on the phone getting agitated. Ray wanted to see Dylan but neither Sam nor I wanted him round here. I said quietly.

'What about your Mum's?'
Sam nodded and said to Ray. 'I'll be at Mum's from four o'clock this afternoon if you want to see Dylan, come there.' And put the phone down so he couldn't answer her.

'You know that I was only ever meant to be an affair. To my shame I was happy with that. I never wanted Ray full time,' Sam said to me one evening. 'I never even wanted to be a mistress, I didn't set out to steal someone else's husband, but I fell for Ray's charms. I didn't let myself think how much you might be hurt by it all.'

'What hurt me most was Dylan. Ray and I had put off having children, which I was in full agreement with to start with but as we got better off I wanted to start a family. Ray kept saying, not yet. So, I left it. Dylan coming along was what hurt most.'

Watching the little boy trying out his crawl across the room. Sam said. 'He wasn't meant to be. He was not in the picture at all. But I made a mistake. My fault. I nearly got rid of him, wasn't going to tell Ray. But I couldn't and had to tell him I was pregnant. He was good and found a house for us to rent. He would come round as often as he could, and he loves Dylan. Even then Ray wanted to keep it from you, and it was only when you found out about us that he moved in with me. It takes two to make or break a relationship though doesn't it?'

'Or Maybe three?' I said indicating the little bundle slowly making his way toward the television.

'Yes, I think you're right, Ray and I would have split in time and you two would still be married. You'd never have known about us. But for Dylan.'

I thought, I would never have gone to Rimini either.

Two weeks to the day that Sam moved in Charley borrowed a van and took all their stuff to her Mum's house. He stayed there all afternoon helping her get everything in and came back with a huge smile on his face.

I missed them, although the house had been a bit too full, and I got the feeling that Charley missed them more. What was it with that girl and my family? I wondered. But this time she was free and so was Charley. In that two weeks he fell in love with that little boy. And I think with Sam.

At least Ray seemed to have got the hint and was no longer angling to come back. I had never seen him so angry as he was that day. He had no right to be angry as he was the one that caused the whole scenario in the first place. He apologised and knew he was wrong with all that my wife, my house stuff. I met him for coffee one morning in town. He apologised so many times, I thought I could do with a pound for each one and he would have to file for bankruptcy. In the end I told him to stop saying sorry, and just get it through his head that I will not have him back under any circumstances. There would be no rekindling of our relationship, our failed marriage. It wasn't as if it was that good in the first place.

'Well, if it had been you would never have gone off with Sam, would you?'

'Oh' I'm so sorry.' he said again.

'Just stop with the apologising and anyway I think maybe you may have done Charley a favour.'

'Really?'

'He seems to be spending an inordinate amount of time round there,' I said.

I haven't seen Ray laugh so much for several years. 'Well that serves me right doesn't it?' he chortled. That's more like the Ray I always knew. Not the obsessive, overgrown child he'd been lately. The affable charming amusing man seemed to have returned.

'Do you still want me to buy you out?' he asked. 'I won't lie, it will put a strain on the finances.'

'If it'll be difficult then, no. That was just anger talking. I'm still happy to take a dividend income. Really that way it's easier for me to work out my tax. I said that in the heat of the moment. But our relationship is purely business from now on. Right?'

'Yes, business and friends? By the way I really think you could do with getting a more up to date computer for your company. Especially as you now have your posh new studio. It all looks good and very professional by the way. We should have thought about doing that ages ago. Even at the sacrifice of my beloved summer house,' he said smiling. Knowing that he'd been wanting to pull it down and put a greenhouse there.

'But I'm being let down by my old steam driven computer? Well I could do with one but nothing too expensive.'

'I'll look into it for you if you like, and mates' rates, I

should be able to do you a good deal. With your partners discount as well.'

'That's better, more like the Ray we all know and love,' I said.

Chapter 20
Pieta

Well the time had come. Maria, Mamma and I were at the airport going to England. I had been chatting with George all week and he'd arranged accommodation for me in a hotel close to the distributing works.

Maria was to be met at the London side by her parents, I was to hire a car and drop Mamma off at home then go on to the hotel George had arranged. He said he'd meet me there tonight with Jess. But it is not all work I'd be able to have a holiday as well. Although I've never driven in England, I was sure I'd get used to it in no time. I just had to remember that I should be on the side of the white line although on the wrong side of the road. Strange people these English.

The flight had been uneventful and gathering our cases we left the airport to be greeted by Maria's parents. They were introduced and seemed overjoyed to have her home. Maria and I kissed goodbye fondly. I found a seat in the coffee shop for Mamma to look after the bags while I went to the car hire desk. Something big enough for her luggage and my small case. But comfortable and easy to drive. They had a nice saloon car the same model as the one I had at home. That way I only had to get used to having the steering wheel on the wrong side. After dropping Mamma off and popping in to have tea with my lovely Auntie. I headed for the hotel. Not quite to the standard of my own but good enough. It was a kind of up market motel. After all I was only sleeping here.

A quick shower to clean the travel dust off and I'd go to the attached restaurant across the car park to meet with George and Jess.

Fran

Jess had told me to get dressed up as she and George were taking me out to dinner. But not too dressy as we were not going anywhere posh. Just a hotel side restaurant. Burger joint, as Jess called it. She could be such a contradiction sometimes. I know she loves popping in those restaurants. So, the silk shirt and jeans could have another airing. I wondered why they wanted to take me out. Was there an announcement? Were they moving in together? George's distribution plant is coming along nicely by all accounts and I'm sure he's thinking of relocating himself soon. He had managers for all his shops and could keep control from his new offices at the centre. The Italian wines should be arriving soon, and I still had the labels to finalise for Pieta's wines. The work was all done, just need them to be signed off.

George had asked me to do some for the other wine growers who are willing to have their labels changed as well. It was a good commission and has proved quite lucrative. Talking of Labels.

'Oh, and George asked if you can bring the labels with you? He wants to have another look at them before they are sent off to be printed. What's the word? Oh, finalised.' Jess said when she phoned me with final instructions. 'We'll see you there at half past seven. Okay?'

'Yes, fine.' I was still quite confused but thought I might as well do as I'm told. After all there was no arguing with Jess when she is on a mission. Whatever that mission was.

As I pulled into the car park, I noticed Jess and George had also just arrived, so we walked in together. He went to the desk and gave his name and we were shown to a table. There was someone already sitting down. I thought, I know that hair the way it curled over the collar of his shirt, that build. The set of his shoulders, my breath came in short gasps. It couldn't be, could it? I was rooted to the spot until Jess gave me a push. He got up, turned and the biggest smile appeared on his face. A smile I remembered so well, so dear to me.

'Pieta,' I squeaked. I wasn't dreaming, He was here, right in front of me. He was still smiling but looking a bit less confident. Not all distant and severe, as he had been in Rimini, but worried, unsure. I was confused. Was he just here to okay the labels? Or something else. My legs went weak and I could feel my heart jumping about all over the place. Why had he come here? That mouth that I so wanted to just kiss was still smiling at me. The smile went right up to his eyes. He was happy to see me. Oh, how I would love to have seen that smile in Rimini.

'Hello Fran.'

'Come on, sit down both of you. I'm starving,' Jess ordered.

I put my folder down and nearly sat on it. Not very professional for a presentation of my work. I found it hard to talk. My heart was jumping about, and I could hear it loud in my ears. I was sure the rest of the restaurant could hear it as well.

Pieta took my hand and plonked himself down next to me. I could feel his heartbeat through his hand. He must be feeling the same.

'How come you're here?' I finally asked, getting my voice to work again.

'I had to come to give my consent to the labels,' He said looking at me so hard that I felt his eyes boring down into my soul.

'All this way? You could have done it by email.'

'Did you not want me to come? Was this a mistake? I can go home?'

'No, no, no, I have to talk to you, I tried in Italy but ….' I tailed off.

Jess and George went to the bar to order drinks. Well to leave us alone for a while anyway.

Well there was only one thing I wanted to clear up and had to say it straight away before I lost my voice all together.

'My mother had kept your letters from me. I never received them. She still had them, and she gave them to me a few months ago. They were lovely, and I am so sorry that I didn't get the chance to reply to them.' I was breaking down now and I couldn't go on. But the relief I saw on Pieta's face was enough to reassure me.

'I knew there must be a reason. But Fran. How do you feel now? Do I still have a chance? You married but I have since heard of your divorce?'

'Yes, I married, but not now. Not anymore.'

Jess and George returned to the table. We ordered food, but I couldn't eat very much. I didn't want to be here with all these people I wanted to be alone with Pieta. To talk and explain. And to kiss him.

After we'd eaten, we took a quick look at the labels. George and Pieta both agreed that they looked the part and would do well on Pieta's bottles for the English market. Then Jess, looked at her watch and said

'I have to go. I have stuff to do. Have you finished George? You know what they say? Time waits for no man. That's a really old one by the way, so old no-one knows the origin of it.'

Pieta looked confused so I explained. 'It's a saying and Jess knows where they all come from. She's made a study of it. You can stop being so obvious, Jess,' I said

'And, yes, I'm staying here for a while to talk with Pieta, if that is alright with you?' I said looking straight at him.

'That's very alright with me,' he answered squeezing my hand.

Well, what can I say? We didn't stay very long in the restaurant after Jess and George had departed for their all-important thing they had to do. We made our way through the hotel to Pieta's room. And there was not much talking done for a while. I did try.

'I expect you thought you'd got rid of me again when I came home last time.'

'Missed you more like. Oh, so much. Mamma kept me from you. She saw your ring and that was it. She whisked me away.'

Then he kissed me, and I went rather weak at the knees. The current running between us was enough to tell me that he still had the same feeling for me as I had for him. All talking stopped for a while and we just explored each other's bodies. I have never felt like this, I just wanted to mould myself into his shape. Oh, I had waited so long for this.

Pieta

Oh, I'd waited so long for this. I'm not the most experienced of lovers, but it felt so good, so right. My first love and now I know my only love. What a night. We'll talk later but right now I am just loving the feel of her body against mine. Safe to say Fran didn't go home that night. She was still with me in the morning. We did talk much later. We told each other everything about our lives. Now we know it all and why we'd not been able to be this happy.

Fran

I woke in Pieta's embrace. And I smiled. A genuine smile. When I opened my eyes, he was just looking directly at me.

'Oh, I must look a state, I bet all my makeup is smudged all over my face.'
He nodded.   'Yes, it is. And my hair will also be all over the place.'
I nodded.   'Yes, it is.'
'Breakfast? Or?'
'Definitely or,' I said
And we made love again.
When we arrived back at my house, I showed Pieta my studio and left him to make some coffee while I went to have a shower and get the rest of my makeup off. The hotel soap had been useful to wash my face but left me with black panda eyes.

'When do you have to go back to Italy?' I asked.

'I have a week. Can you take some time off and show me your home?'

'I can indeed.' I said thinking to myself that I have to get in touch with some of my customers and tell them there may be a bit of a delay. Nothing was urgent so I'm sure they'll understand that I have to take some time off work. They'll wait.

What a week we had. I took him to meet Mum and Michael. Well Mum properly that is. I took him to see Dad and Sheila. We went out walking in lovely country parks and I showed him the English countryside. We went to quaint pubs and he tried English bitter. He wasn't keen. We talked and talked and kissed a lot. And each night either at my house or if Charley was home, at his hotel, we made love. Everything was perfect for me. I have never been so happy. We went to the local stables where I had learned to ride as a child and rode out. Pieta told me about his horses and how he tries to ride them often, but time is precious.

'When you went home that first time and I wrote those letters to you. I thought that you'd changed your mind about the Italian lad. That you got home and put it down to a holiday romance and forgot all about me. I could never free my heart to find another and so I stayed single. Although I have to say most of my life has been work so there really was no spare time for romance. When you came back, and I saw your wedding ring I knew then that I had been right. That you had been just enjoying a holiday romance.'

'When I came home, and I didn't hear from you I thought that getting English girls address was some kind of trophy. So, I tried to put you to the back of my mind and just got on with my life. I met Ray soon after coming home from that holiday. I'm still angry at my interfering mother for what she did.'

'You mustn't blame your Mother. She did what she thought was best. As well as mine this year. We've found each other now. It is not too late for us. You will come to Italy? Be with me? I need you there with me Fran.'

'Oh yes Pieta, I want to be with you, I will, I'll find a way. There's so much to think about. But, yes Pieta, yes I will come to Italy to be with you.'

We then went to see his Mother. She was quite cool towards me at first, but soon thawed when she realised how much in love we were.

'So, is it to be a spring wedding? Will it be here or in Italy? So much to organise. So much to do.'
His Auntie was over the moon,

'Oh, another wedding. I do love a good wedding.'

'We have to think about all that Mamma, Pieta said to

her. 'We have plenty of time.'

Then my Pieta had to go home to Italy. He couldn't stay here any longer. I'll miss having him here with me but at least I know we'll be together, that he still loves me and Oh, how I love him. I'm going out there in a few weeks to meet and get to know the rest of his family.

Mamma Bianchi is coming with me. That is unfortunately unavoidable. She has insisted. Who am I to disagree?

I talked to him daily either face time, skype, or we even actually phoned each other sometimes. Feeling so happy I couldn't wait to get there and enjoy my new life. Once I've met the rest of the family that is, which was rather a big deal for me. I wondered how they'd take me. The English girl who broke his heart all those years ago. Would they hold it against me? There was no way he could move to England so if we were to be together, I must move to his home. Leave mine. It would be a bit of a wrench, but I know where I wanted to be. With Pieta.

Chapter 21

Fran

Now I had to get some of my workload cleared up and find a space in my ever-filling diary to have a break in Italy. Jess was over the moon that her little plan worked. She knew that if she could just get us together for long enough, we'd be able to work it all out. Clear up the misunderstandings and see if there was still anything there for us. Well she was right. And she was preening, becoming quite unbearable. She kept saying 'Told you so.' There was no need to wait, I knew Pieta was the man for me and I wanted to spend the rest of my life with him.

'I am going to up sticks and move there to be with him,' I told her.

'You are taking all your furniture? she asked. 'The phrase can have a few meanings, moving to a new house furniture and all or could be about raising the mast of a ship.'

'I'm glad you told me that.' I'll be taking my plan-chest and some of those bits of Grandma's. Pieta is going to build me a completely new studio.'

'What, you moving that bloody thing again? It's happy where it is. After all the time it took us to get it downstairs.'

But what to do with the house? The sensible thing to do would be to rent it out. Complete with my studio that I'd so enjoyed using. But should I put it with an agent? If so which one? There's so much involved with moving to another country. I'm wasn't going to let fear of the unknown put me off or stop me. I'm wouldn't be alone when I got there, there was Pieta and all his family. Or should I sell the house? Or do as Pieta suggested and leave it empty, so we'd have somewhere to stay. I'd have to brush up on my poor schoolgirl Italian, but Mamma Bianchi had said she'll give me some lessons. I got to see quite a lot of her, not so much taken me under her wing as dominated my free time. But I didn't mind. It was all for the good. There's so much I had to learn about the Italian culture and how to behave as the wife of an Italian man.

There were a few minor problems to sort out first. It'd be some weeks before I could get there. Not till the end of the next month at least. But the good thing about that was Pieta shouldn't be so busy. I think it's what they called a shoulder season in the trade. That's not high season but the in between bits. There'll be a spike at Christmas time but once the English October half term is over the amount of people from here flying to Italy is less. Although Pieta says they do get some from more northern countries coming at that time of the year and couples, not so many families.

So, he says he'd be able to take some time off and show me around. I had commissions to finish but it was hard to concentrate, all I wanted to think about was getting to Italy. I'd been like a teenager all over again. High on love. Although time seemed to be creeping along it was amazing how long it was since Pieta went home. Several weeks have gone by and for some reason when I was checking my diary, I noticed that one date in particular was not noted. I flicked back to count how long since I last entered it. Nearly six weeks. My period. I haven't marked a date for that. I've missed one. Oh! Oh gosh! Could I be pregnant? I really didn't know what to think. I'd been sitting down counting days again and again. Trying to work out how long it had been. It would seem that that if I was pregnant it happened around the first night Pieta and I spent together. I hadn't noticed any odd cravings, but I did think I had better drop some of this weight as my bras had been feeling a bit snug. My head was in a whirl, what was I to do? How would Pieta take it? Would he think I was trying to trap him into marriage? We had never mentioned getting married even though Mamma Bianchi was preparing for a wedding. So, while I was out shopping, I picked up some pregnancy test kits. Five of them. From five different chemists. Well you do need to be sure of these things, don't you? They are all different makes, and all have separate ways to tell you if you are pregnant or not. Some have one blue line, some two. Some pink lines and some just have the word pregnant. It was going to take me a while to get all these wet and tested.

'I'll have a couple of pints of water and make a start.' I told myself. I did a lot of that, talking to myself back then, especially when I let myself get worried. When I spoke to Pieta on Facetime, I didn't mention any of it to him. I tried to keep up a general conversation. I asked him how everything was going that end and we set plans for a time for me to travel out there.

  I decided after reading the instructions that I'd better wait until the morning to do the tests. So, first thing, one after the other in the stream they went. I put them on a tissue on the sink top and waited. I could hardly wait even the two minutes and kept picking them up in turn to see if I could distinguish the result. Go and make some coffee, I thought. When you come back, they should reveal the awful truth. But I couldn't take my eyes off them. Eventually they started to show themselves to me. The writing or lines began to show in the little windows. All five of them indicated the same.

Positive. Every single one of them said the same loud and clear. Positive.

When Jess popped round a bit later, I was standing in the kitchen looking at the results of five kits all saying the same. Stunned. Yes, pregnant!

'What's up?' she asked as she walked in.

I just pointed to the kits lined up on the work top.

'Oops!' was all she said. 'You're pregnant? How does Pieta feel about this?'

'I haven't told him yet, I only just did them. You are the only person besides me that does know.'

'Don't look so worried, I'm sure he'll be delighted.'

'Will he? I hope so, but I don't want him thinking I am trying to trap him.'

'Trap him? Why would he think that? He wants you to go live with him, doesn't he? Found the love of his life again, he said. Couldn't be happier, he told George. Why should he not want to be trapped?'

'He's never asked me to marry him.'

'But his mother is busy buying outfits for your wedding, isn't she?'

'Yes, she is running around like the proverbial blue fly. In fact, she is taking me to look at wedding dresses. For, you understand, second time rounders. Not white, she says, it would not be proper, as she puts it. How will she take this? She can easily start trying to part us. She has only just come around to liking me.'

'She'll be fine and if it makes her Pieta happy, she will be happy. You know that. And you know what they say? A baby fills a space in your heart that you never knew was empty. Source unknown by the way.'

'You think so?'

'I know so.'

'I'll tell him when we next facetime. Oh Jess, I am so

scared. Children, I never thought I'd be able to have any of those and I'm going to be bringing this one up in a foreign country. That's if Pieta and his mother are happy about it.'

'Well, I'm sure she'll tell you exactly what the protocol is. She will be ecstatic having another grandchild and I suspect you won't be doing much of the looking after, when she's there. You'll be lucky to get a look in.' Tears sprang to my eyes and they were accompanied by laughter. Oh, what a mess, I thought I had my life all planned out. But all my plans went to pot a couple of years ago when Ray walked out. So, I should stick that virtual rod up my back and just get on with all this and accept that things come along sometimes to knock us off course.

'Well I was going to open a bottle to celebrate the sales of Pieta's wine but as you can't drink. We'd better have a cup of coffee. Or are you off that? I can make some tea?'

'I haven't noticed any strange food fads, well not yet anyway.'

'No eating coals or charcoal? Ice cubes dipped in pickle? Banana and mustard sandwiches?'

'Oh, shut up. They would really turn my stomach. Oh Jess, how exciting is this? I'm all conflusterated, which isn't a word I know but that's me at the moment. Excited and scared, so bloody scared.'

'Well, coffee it is. What time are you talking to Pieta?'

'About three our time, he has a bit of a slow period then. Oh God, how will he take it? What if he is angry or upset? We've talked about all sorts but haven't mentioned children. What if he doesn't want any? Or wants to wait?'

'Takes two my dear, and it's just as much his

responsibility as yours, so he has no right to be angry or upset. And Mamma Bianchi wants more grandchildren, doesn't she?'

'But what if he is? What if he's angry or upset?'

'Then you've spent the last few months wasting your time on an idiot.'

'Jess, he isn't that.'

'No? So why are you worried?'

Jess decided she'd better stay until after the facetime call, just in case I needed her, but she really thought I was being silly.

I'm just so scared about telling him. I've only just found out myself and still getting used to the idea. After all these years waiting and wanting, it's going to happen, and now I am very frightened. Am I too old? Will I be able to cope? And most of all how will I cope if Pieta doesn't want a child and leaves me to bring it up by myself? How will I tell him? Oh goodness there is my phone.' I do have a propensity to run on a bit when I'm nervous.

'Hello, my Adorato, how are you today?' Then I saw his face fall into concern. 'My love whatever is wrong, why are you crying?'

I couldn't help myself, I was very emotional, was it hormones? Can they do that? Can they just make you cry at the drop of a hat?

'Oh Pieta, I have something to tell you.' The easy smile dropped further from his face, his beloved face. He was immediately worried.

'My darling, whatever it is we can deal with it. Unless you want to...'

He couldn't finish the sentence.

'No, No, nothing like that. Oh Pieta. I don't know. I don't know how to tell you this.'

Jess couldn't contain herself any longer. She piped up from the background.

'Pieta, she's pregnant. She is having your baby.'

His face went from worried to absolute joy in the space of half a second.

'Oh, my darling, that is wonderful. I am to be a Papa? Oh, you are such a clever girl. How I wish I could be with you to hug you.'

I was so relieved; I had been worrying so much all morning. 'Really? I asked. You're pleased? Oh, I'm so glad.'

'Of course, my love I am so happy, this is fantastic. Marvellous. Oh, my wonderful girl. Oh, I love you and now there will be two to love.'

Jess was sitting in the corner smiling as we continued our conversation with that satisfied look on her face. I was just waiting for her to say, 'told you.' Eventually Pieta ran out of wonderful things to say and had to get back to work.

'Will I tell Mamma?' he asked before we said goodbye.'

I sighed and said with relief,

'Yes, you do that. It will come better from you.'

Pieta

Fran seemed to be so very nervous at telling me about the baby, but I couldn't be happier. It was a strange feeling, that one that I was going to be a father. I'd been responsible for many people in my life but now I had Fran and our child. That's real responsibility. Although I felt the weight of that on my shoulders, I had an inner contentment. Life was just getting better all the time. I had the love of my life back in it and now we were bringing new life into our happy world. I couldn't believe my lucky stars, and how my world had shifted in to such a happy place.

I wanted to be with her and share the excitement of this pregnancy with her. The timing could have been better but at least we'd have time to get used to the idea. I had to tell someone. Mamma, of course and Guilia, and Bella. I was like a child opening Christmas presents. I have fathered a child. I just remembered something I still had to do. Put Fran's beach scene painting back up on my office wall. I don't know why I didn't do it as soon as I came home, but it didn't feel right until this moment. Now I knew and am certain that we would be together. All of us.

I picked up the phone, Mamma first of course.

'Mamma, how are you?'

'Pieta, this is not a usual time for you to call. What? You have something to tell me, I just know it, something terrible has happened.'

'That depends on how you look at it. I have news.'

'Is this good news? Or are you going to tell me something horrible?'

'It is very good news Mamma. Fran is expecting, and we are going to be parents.'

'Oh, oh I see.'

'You don't sound very happy for me Mamma?'

'Very soon, are you sure this is good?'

'Believe me Mamma, it is good. Be happy for me, I know I've been a disappointment to you but now you are to have another grandchild. You wanted that didn't you?'

'Never a disappointment but this is very sudden, and you hardly know her.'

'I know all I need to know, and I hardly knew Maria,

but you'd have been happy for it to happen with her. All I need to know about Fran is that I have always loved her and will love my child.'

'I will go and see Fran and be happy for her and you. Yes, I'll go and see her.'

Well, not quite the reaction I expected from Mamma, but I suppose I did rather hit her with it. But I've never been one to talk around something, if I have something to say I'll just say it. Mamma should know that by now. I hope she's a bit gentler with Fran. Now to tell my sisters, they I'm sure will be happy for me. I took the painting out from my drawer and went to put it back on the wall, in its spot, then turned to reach for the phone.

But before I could get to the phone again Guilia was calling me. So, Mamma had already got to her and was no doubt calling Bella right now.

'Congratulations big brother, so you are to be a father?'

'Mamma was quick off the mark. I was then going to ring you.'

'She is really excited. She is talking to Bella now.'

'Oh, she didn't seem to be pleased when I spoke to her.'

'You just took her by surprise, she is probably already planning shopping trips to buy the baby clothes and cots and everything.'

'Oh, dear, I suppose she'll swamp poor Fran. I need to be there to protect her from Mamma.'

'Well, Fran has one as well, a mother that is, so Mamma will have to take her turn. But yes, you need to be there, and you should go as soon as you can.'

'Yes, I want to, but have things to organise first.'

'No, just go. Leave lists, instructions, whatever but just go.'

Fran

Jess stayed with me for the rest of the afternoon, while I phoned Mum and told her. She was a bit perturbed, but she could tell it was making me very happy. She soon decided she was able to be happy about it.

'So, at last you are going to make me a grandmother. I'll have to be popping over to Italy even more often now, won't I?'

'Yes, Mum you can come over and baby sit as often as you like,' I laughed.

'Will you be alright to travel?'

'I'll take the doctor's advice about flying, don't worry. I won't do anything to upset either of us. Not having waited for so long.'

Then I phoned Dad, well not Dad as he was still at work. But Sheila answered and was full of encouragement. She said much the same about coming to Italy more often than they'd at first thought about. She said did I want her to tell Dad when he came in or should she get him to ring me? I said I'd love to tell him, so he'll be ringing at some time around six this evening.

'Are you sitting down? I asked him.

'Oh, do I need to?' he said sounding a bit nervous.

'Might be a good idea.'

'Okay, I'm sitting, what is it that you have to tell me? He sounded rather worried.

'Don't worry I'm not filing for bankruptcy, or anything like that. I'm not ill but, I am pregnant. You are going to be a grand dad.'

'Oh, really? Phew! I really thought you were going to tell me something awful then. How long must I wait?'

'Quite a while I only just found out, and well you can

work it out for yourself. Pieta was here mid-September so I'm only about 6 weeks gone.'

'You're going over there, soon aren't you? Had you better delay that do you think? Sheila says the first three months are the most dangerous.'
So, Sheila had already told him.

'I'll see what the doctor says about it. But I can't see there being a problem. I'm pretty healthy.'

'Well, congratulations my darling. You'll make a fantastic mother.'
After a while we hung up and almost immediately there was a knock on the door. Charley was in by that time, so he went to answer it. In came this whirling dervish of a future mother-in-law.

'You must rest, more. Charley go and make this poor girl a cup of your English tea. Sit, my dear, you have to take care of yourself. I will make sure you do that. You need your rest. I will be here daily to make sure you are getting enough rest. I shall not let anything happen to this child. Or you my dear,' she added as an afterthought.

I decided that I'd better do as I was told and let her look after me. But I did point out to her that I have to work for a living. There was no way around that. And that I did have a mother of my own who would also want to be here.

Mamma Bianchi spent the next few days bossing everyone about and trying to wrap me in her very own protective blanket. I fully expected a roll of bubble wrap to be delivered any time, so that I didn't hurt myself. Every day either my mother or Mamma was there making sure I didn't overdo it, both together sometimes, sparking off each other. Although they did allow that I had to go to work and still go out once in a while. In the end I had to ask Pieta to ask his mum to back off a bit and I had a similar conversation with my mother.

'You don't want me here? How do you think you are going to cope if I am not here to help you?' Mamma asked.

'Well, I am able to be here sometimes you know,' Mum said to her. Oh, dear a fight between grandmothers was going to break out any minute.

'Why don't you take it in turns to come round?' I said. Then I built up my courage and said, 'One afternoon a week each.'

'What?' They both said at the same time.

'That's what I said, I am not dying, nor am I ill, I am having a baby, that's all.'

'That's all?' again from both of them.

'Yes, all. I love having you round here, and you can both come together one day as well, but I do need some time to myself. After all I have work to do, and when was the last time I had a conversation with Pieta without one of you being here? Or Charley for that matter.'

'Charley, he should not be here, it is not fitting, A man should not live here with you alone while your future husband is all the way back home in Italy.'

'Oh, don't be silly, they're more or less cousins,' Mum told her.

'Charley is my lodger,' I said by this time I was getting a bit annoyed. 'Now, both of you go, I will see Mamma on Monday and Mum on Wednesday and both of you can come on Friday. There, it is all arranged.'

'What about over the weekend?'

'Mamma, I still have friends, There's Claire, Sue and Sandra. I often see Jess on Saturday and maybe I will go out with her. You know for must haves.'

Mamma looked puzzled. 'What?'

Mum patted her arm and said 'Shopping.'

'Ah, that I understand.'

Both of them looked very unhappy about the arrangement but they could see I was adamant and went away chattering to each other about the ungrateful younger generation. I had a quiet sit, all alone, and face timed Pieta. All those times I'd worried about being left alone and now all I craved was a bit of peace and quiet.

'So, how did it go, the telling of the collective Mamma's?' Pieta asked.

'Well, it was a bit scary but not too bad, they'll get over it, but it's so nice to have some time to myself and to be able to talk to you without one of them peering over my shoulder.'

'And for me, to get you alone. You are keeping well? I can hardly wait for you to get here. So long to wait, I want to hold you and kiss every growing inch of you.'

Oh, Pieta, you know just how to make me feel better.

'Well I have an appointment with the doctor tomorrow. Just to confirm everything and book a scan. I'll call when I've been there and let you know how it goes.'

'Take good care of yourself my darling, I want you both here as soon as possible. Then I can do all the taking care and not leave it to the Mammas.'

'I can't wait to come over and meet the rest of your family. Then I have to decide what to do with this house.'

'Well, there are options. You could rent it out, or keep it empty so we have somewhere to stay when we are visiting? Or sell up, whatever is the least stressful for you? But really you don't have to think about it at all right now.'

'No, you're right. That decision can be left for a while. I just want to be with you. Are you very busy? At the hotel I mean.'

'It is slowing a bit as we're between seasons. Still quite busy but bookings are slowing down now. '

'Good, so you can get some rest then, because you're going to be very busy when baby and I arrive there.' We talked for a few more minutes and then Pieta was needed so he had to go. I hadn't noticed Charley coming in, I was surprised because I thought he was working late today. But obviously I had my days mixed up. Hormones again? That's happening so much lately. Another good reason for taking my life back from Mum and Mamma Bianchi. The weight of their constant presence has lifted, I've had time to think and let my poor beleaguered brain a rest.

'Can I have a word?' he asked. He looked rather serious. I wondered what was wrong.

'Of course. What's up?'

'Nothing to bad, well that kind of depends on how you see it though.'

'You're getting me worried now. Whatever is it?'

'Well, you know I took Sam and Dylan to her Mum's?'

'Yes, I saw you go. What of it?'

'I've seen her since then, in fact I have been seeing her.'

I had an inward chuckle but kept my face serious. I had wondered if it was Sam, he was going out to see all these weeks. I did think to myself that there had been an attraction there.

'Oh, have you?' I said.

'Um, yes.'

'Are you telling me you're moving out?'

'No. Rather, that we'd like to move in, when you go to Italy that is. I could pay you a fair rent and this house would make a perfect family home.

'Blimey, you haven't wasted any time, have you?'

'Just one of those things. I actually stayed around to help her get back on her feet after Ray. She and I sort of, well you know.'

'Charley? What are you trying to say? What don't I know about this? You have been seeing her all of about a couple of months, and you are moving in together?'

'No, no she isn't pregnant.' But we do really get on well, I love Dylan and I love her. I think she loves me; I hope so.'

'Well, I got to know Sam quite well while she and Dylan were here, and she's a nice girl. Even if she did steal my husband. But as Jess is so fond of saying, it takes two.'

'So, you aren't angry with us then?'

'Angry? Who am I to stand in the way of true love?' I said flinging my arms round him.

'Although, Sam does seem to have a preference for the men in my life. But would she be happy living here, knowing that it was my home with Ray?'

'She says she thinks she'd be okay with it. We've discussed it and if we could decorate it differently, we could sort of make it ours. Seemingly, she does seem to find joy in your family. Now what are we going to have for dinner? I'll cook. You haven't got any cravings, yet have you? Or anything you simply can't eat?'

'Ha ha, no I'm fine with all food at the moment.' And off he went to the kitchen to rustle up a feast for us. No wonder Sam liked him.

Chapter 22.

Fran.

My first visit to the doctors since the pregnancy was confirmed. He was a bit worried about me flying before I am twelve weeks into the pregnancy. I'll have a scan at about then to make sure everything is alright as an older first-time mother. The scan was booked in for the last week of November, and I had arranged my flight to Italy a week after that. So, it wouldn't be until December that I can get to Pieta. Oh, dear it seems such a long wait. He was here in September and now I have to wait all this time.

'Better to be safe than sorry,' my mother said to me. Always one for the clichés. Jess would tell me just where that one came from. But this time she's right, I just had to be sensible, hard as it was. But I did so want to get to Italy to see my lovely man. I'd been composing a letter to send to all my existing customers, informing them of the move to Italy and that I would be available for work from a distance. I've told them I can still take on commissions for the time being. But will be taking maternity leave some weeks before I set off. I had too many other things to think about. Mamma Bianchi had changed her flight, so she was able come with me and she'd stay over Christmas, it's not worth her coming home just to fly out again a couple of weeks later. I did love her and her kindness and consideration, but I would rather have gone alone. Oh well.

I woke on the day of the scan feeling a bit nervous. I'd told Mum and Mamma that Jess was coming with me, only a little lie, I didn't want them both fussing about, but just as I was eating a bit of dry toast the doorbell rang. There he was, my Italian man, complete with a suitcase and a bunch of flowers so big I could hardly see him behind them.

'Pieta,' I squealed. And flowers or no flowers I jumped straight into his arms. What a surprise.

'I couldn't wait, I wanted to be here to take you for the scan, I wanted to see you and our baby.'

'I'm so glad you're here,' I said hugging him so tight I wasn't entirely sure how he kept breathing.

I made him some coffee and told him all about Sam and Charley's visit, so she could see if she would be comfortable living here.

'Sam was a bit unsure about living in the house Ray had so easily walked out of. But she couldn't deny that it would be very convenient, and I told her she could decorate just how she wanted. She seemed more convinced by the time they'd left, and they both went away with a smile on their faces.'

Pieta nodded and said that it sounded like a good plan.

It seemed as if everything was coming together so well. Was it meant to be? I think at last my life was going in a direction that I liked. I need not have worried about Pieta's reaction to the baby, he was as excited as me. And I just wanted to kiss that lovely smiling face. So, after many kisses and hugs we set out to the hospital for the scan, for the first sight of our baby. Of course, he wanted to be there.

'This will be cold,' the sonographer said as she squirted gel on to my tummy. Then she turned to the machine, fiddled with a few knobs and said 'Ah, there we are, a nice strong heartbeat. Then she looked at us both and I thought she was going to say something terrible, as a look of consternation came across her face.

'I have two here.'

'Two what?' Pieta asked looking worried.

'Two what, heartbeats?' I asked.
She nodded.' Yes, two heartbeats. Congratulations you are having twins. Not unexpected, they can be a bit more, er, common in the slightly older Mum. Especially a first pregnancy.'
It was a good job I was already sitting, or I should say laying down.

'Twins? Are you sure?' Breathing a sigh of relief. I had thought she was going to say something horrible, but two babies. We're going to have two babies.

'I'll print off the scan but of course you can have a three D scan, if you like, a bit further on in the pregnancy.'
Pieta and I looked at each other and all be it we were in a certain amount of shock we just smiled.

'So, my family is complete?'

'Life just keeps throwing me these great big bites of happiness right now, I just don't believe that it can be this good,' I said.

'It is a good job I'm here to look after you,' he told me.
We both were on cloud nine we walked out of the hospital and drove home. Pieta made me sit down and went to make some tea. I was still in shock when both mothers arrived to see the scan pictures. We'd made sure we got plenty of copies as we knew we'd be needing them.

'What is that? I can't make out the baby's shape,' Mamma asked.
My mum just looked at me and smiled. She had seen the two babies.

'There's two in there.'
Both the mothers went into their own conversation totally ignoring the fact that Pieta and I were there. They had decided that I could not possibly fly to Italy

until I was at least six months. They then went on to organise how they were going to look after me while I was waiting to get to Italy. We were not even involved in this conversation, so Pieta and I left them to it and went for a short walk around the estate. We stopped in a coffee shop for a sit down

'I will have to see what the doctor says about when I can fly,' I said

'That would be the best, when are you going again?'

'I have an appointment during the week. How long can you stay?'

He smiled. 'Long enough. I can come with you, if you like.'

Do I like? I couldn't be more overjoyed.

For all the worrying that the two mothers had done, the doctor was happy for me to fly the following week. Pieta arranged his flight to coincide with mine, and I got to work finishing up all the last dregs of this year's workload. I'd not be doing any more until after the Christmas holidays. I wanted to be home for Christmas, possibly a last English one. Then I had to knuckle down and get some more commissions finished off. At least with my job there isn't much in the way of heavy lifting. Mainly sitting which even now is not so comfortable as it was. I had about two weeks to relax in Italy. Well I didn't think it was going to be that relaxing as I still had the ordeal to go through of meeting the sisters and their husbands. How would they take to me, would they resent me because I broke their brothers' heart all those years ago? It worried me and although Pieta tried to sooth my nerves and said that the worst one to get round was his mother, and that I had her wrapped around my little finger, I was still nervous.

Pieta

The time had at last come and it's so welcome., it was time for Fran to get to know the rest of my family and for them to meet my heart's desire. I knew they'd love her as much as I do. Mamma was the first step and she's already enamoured with her. Bella and Guilia would be as well, I was sure. They just wanted to get their hands on the bambini. I had to keep pinching myself. This was real, I was going to be a father and I had the woman I'd wanted for so many years coming to be with me. It just seemed too good to be true after all this time. I can still remember my sadness when I had no replies to my letters. The jolt of pain and joy when I saw her again. Mamma's manipulation to keep us apart and finally the utter euphoria when Fran said that she had loved me and still did.

We were to fly out the next week, and Fran has said she would like to stay in the hotel for some of the time then go to the farm. That's a good plan, there is so much I want to show her and plan with her. Mamma can have a great time showing Fran around her friends there. Bella and Guilia also, will be able to show her off. Then I can have her to myself for a while.

Fran

Pieta was being so gentle with me, I'm sure he thought I'd break if he hugged me too hard. I still couldn't believe we'd be together and that everything was going to work out for us. It didn't seem possible that having found him again we could still feel the same about each other. And twins? I was somewhat nervous of meeting the sisters but if I was to live with him in Italy, I needed to be able to get on with his family there. He said they were excited to meet me.

While I packed Pieta was in my studio taking pictures. He wanted to make sure I had a good set up for when I started work again, in Italy. I'd be able to keep up with my design work and do some painting as well. That's something I've not had time to do much of lately.

Charley and Sam would be moving into this house when I finally leave for Italy, I really thought they may get married when Sam and Ray are divorced. I was pleased that they'll be living here even though it didn't give Pieta and myself somewhere to stay when we came to England. Which he had promised we'd be able to do a lot of. It would be unrealistic to expect everyone to keep flying out to see me. Although I knew Mum and Michael would come often as well as Dad and Sheila. I wondered if there would ever be a time when they could all come together?

Chapter 23

Fran

'The taxi's here,' Jess said looking out of my front window.

'Oh gosh, have I packed everything I need?' I said in my usual going away panic.

'We do have shops in Italy, if you forget something, we will buy it.' Pieta laughed at me.

Slinging my arms around Jess and clinging on as if my life depended on it, I said.

'Thank you so much.'

'Come on now, you'll be back in a couple of weeks, with bags full of Italian designer maternity wear. Look after my God children.'

'Of course, I'll see you in a couple of weeks.' What a rush it's been but finally we're on our way.

'There's Mamma, Pieta said when we met her at the airport, 'Oh God, how much luggage does she need for two weeks?'

'Perhaps she's intending to stay longer.'

Indeed, she was, she had decided to spend Christmas in Italy this year and had brought presents for all the children with her. She told me that as I'd be back in the bosom of my own family for the season she may as well enjoy her own family. I could see she was angling for me to say that I would stay over Christmas. She hoped that I'd leave it too late to fly and then need to stay in Italy for the duration of the pregnancy.

I had come to see how familiar these little games are to all mothers. Just the sort of thing my mother would do. Would I be like that?

'I wonder how your Mother would like an Italian family Christmas,' She mused.

I smiled at Pieta who raised his eyebrows at me behind her back. I just patted her hand and we set about finding a big trolley for all the luggage.

We were able to sit together on the plane, Mamma at the window, then Pieta and I planted myself on the aisle seat, claiming I would need to be able to get to the loo quite often. That two and half hours went in a flash and the moment I had been dreading was upon us. The whole family had turned out to greet us and were in the arrival's hall waiting for our plane. Everyone was talking, hugging, laughing, and such a greeting we had. I couldn't understand a word they were saying; the words came out so quickly, but I knew that I would have to get the hang of this language pretty quickly. Bella spoke some English but Guilia as the youngest of the family had an excellent grasp of the language and of course Mamma and Pieta spoke it perfectly. I would soon learn Italian well enough to converse with everybody.

When we got to the hotel and walked into the reception, the staff that were on duty all turned and applauded us. I felt like we were Royalty. After more greetings and introductions that I would never remember we made our way up in the private lift to Pieta's apartment, so I could rest up a bit and have a clean-up before dinner tonight.

'Blimey, it's huge. We could live here, is that two big bedrooms? En-suit for both?' I peeked in all the rooms. Just to make sure I hadn't missed anything.

'Come and see the roof terrace.' Pieta opened a set of sliding doors to reveal, a complete garden in the sky.

'I thought about putting a fountain up here. What do you think?'

'It's beautiful as it is,' I said.

'You should rest.'

But I didn't want to rest. I really quite fancied a walk on the beach.

'Is there a way we can get out and not be noticed?' I ask Pieta.

'Yes, there's the staff door. Why do you want to go out? I thought you'd want to rest.'

'I want to make memories with you and relive some, down on the beach.'

'It'll be cold down there, not bikini weather,' he smiled. 'Come my Bella, we'll sneak out.'

Having managed to leave without being accosted by any family members we headed for the now deserted beach. No-one sunbathing today. A nippy wind came in off the sea, but I was just loving it. Walking along hand in hand with Pieta. So much at peace, so relaxed and oh so happy. Why had this feeling eluded me for so long? Such simple pleasures, being with the one you love. No talking was necessary, we just meandered along enjoying each other's company. We wandered down to the water's edge and stood looking out to the rough sea. Pieta put a protective arm about my shoulders, and we stood for a long while. Just being. Just together.

Then, in unison we turned and made our way back to the hotel. Where I had a short nap before getting ready for the big family party.

The conversation around the table was in two languages, Bella and Guilia had decided that they would talk and then translate for me. This was just the start of my education.

'Tomorrow we will register you with my doctor, he will check you out to make sure everything is alright,' Mamma said.

'The English doctors have that all in hand Mamma,'

Pieta told her.

'Pah, they may have missed something, I do not trust them.'

I said I would be happy to see her doctor and keep an eye on everything while I'm here.

Bella and Guilia told me they were setting me language lessons to take home, and they would ring or face time me to test me.

'Don't go putting too much pressure on her,' Mamma told them.

'Nonsense,' Bella exclaimed. 'She will need something to do on those cold English winter evenings.'

'Yes, and once home from here Fran may not be able to fly again until the bambini are born,' added Guilia.

'Perhaps, she will stay here?' Mamma questioned.

'I wish I could but there is so much to sort out back home.' I said. 'And I would like one last Christmas with my parents before I become an Italian wife.'

'When are you two going to get married, that's what I want to know?'

'After the babies are born,' Pieta said.

'Yes, I would like my figure back and to be able to toast my new husband with his very own sparkling wine,' I said.

Mamma's pursed lips showed her disapproval of this plan. But she kept quiet. For now. Seeing the disapproving look on her face Pieta said.

'It makes no difference Mamma; we will be married here in Italy after the bambini are born. Fran is my wife in everything but name already. Fran Bianchi. Has a nice ring to it?'

'Will you keep your English name to do your business with?' Guilia asked.

'Well yes, as the company name is established but I'll

change my stationary to reflect my marriage,' I told her.

Pieta

So much was happening in such a small space in time. Were we going too fast? Fran was making a huge step to be here with me, leaving her family, her friends and her home. Learning a whole new language. A new culture. Was I asking too much of her? The babies were a complication, a nice one but still something we needed to be careful of. I so admired her for taking this leap of faith. Faith in me. I hoped it made her as happy as I was right then.

Fran

I knew Pieta was the man for me, but this was all happening so quickly. I didn't know about my feelings for him until I saw him again back in May. Now in December I was carrying his children and we were talking of marriage. The scariest thing was leaving everything I've been so used to back in England and coming here to be with him. His family had welcomed me into his life so warmly. Mamma had wanted a wife for Pieta for so long and for her to accept this English woman must have been be hard for her. I still wondered what would've happened if we'd been able to be together when we were teenagers. Would we still be the same? Still in love? I couldn't answer that, but I did know I was happy and wanted to be with him, even though it meant leaving everything behind. I still stopped short and took a deep breath about how it all came about. Back then, when Jess and I were discussing where to go for our holiday. We both had met people to fill our lives with. There was to be another wedding the following year that Pieta and I would be going to. Jess and George have set a date for September. Pieta and were to take the babies. Mum and Sheila could take turns babysitting while we went to my best friend's wedding. Hopefully I'd have my figure back by then. They'd be coming to Italy for their honeymoon. Two whole weeks.

'September would be a good month for us to make Mamma happy. To become husband and wife,' Pieta said to me one day.

'What are you thinking? Maybe the week after Jess and George's wedding? They'll be in Italy anyway. I'm sure if we give Mum and Dad plenty of notice they can all be here as well.'

'That's what I thought. Shall we? Set a date?'

'Well, at least your Mamma will know what season to buy her outfit for.'

'Yes, that is a very big worry for her. I'll be able to tell her to go for an Autumn wedding, Italian style.'

One fine morning as we wandered around the farm Pieta stopped me and pointed out a tumble-down barn. Not too far from the house.

'This is the building I thought would make a perfect studio for you. I can have it all prepared for when you want to start work again.'

We were by this time staying at the farm after a hectic week of visiting friends and shopping with Mamma, Bella and Guilia for my ever-growing body.

'There's no need for you to look like a ship in full sail,' Bella had said. 'You can have some lovely maternity clothes. Italian design.'

'Oh yes, we know all the best places to buy for you,' Guilia added.

'Pieta will just have to spend some of that money he's been making all these years.

'Yes, none of your dowdy English Stuff. Oh no,' Bella added.

So, we had made quite a few shopping trips. Mamma wanted to buy cots, prams, baby clothes but I asked her to hold off on those, I didn't want to tempt providence.

From the outside this barn looked a bit ramshackle but once inside I could see it was sound and very big,

'You could have your design studio this end and painting the other. We can put windows in the roof and big windows on one side, so it'll be very light. We can run some plumbing from the house for heat and water for your kettle. Just as you do in your garden studio. There's even room for the bambinos to play.'

'Oh, Pieta, it is huge, and so close to the house. Are you sure you want to give it up for my studio?' It would make lovely accommodation.'

'Plenty of other barns to make into accommodation and the house is big enough for when your family want to come to stay. That's if they don't want to stop in the hotel. We can go and see my friend Roman, who is an architect and he can design it just how you want it.'

'It's wonderful. I don't know what to say.'

Pieta knew how much my independence meant to me and that I wanted to keep my company going. He knew I needed something for myself and didn't expect me to just fall into working for him. Ray had considered my company as second to his and just for my pin money. Even though without it he'd never have been able to complete his studies and start his own business.

The next person I was to meet was Roman who visited the farm to measure the building and ask many questions about what I wanted in there. He said he'd have some drawings ready for me very soon. He took the copies of the pictures Pieta had taken of my studio set up. Oh, my goodness, Middleton's Designs Italian studio.

My two weeks in Italy came to a very abrupt early end with a phone call from Mum.

Chapter 24

Fran.

My Dad was only sixty-three years old and I considered him too young to be having a heart attack. But that's what happened. Dad's always been the one constant man in my life, and I relied on him totally. To be there for me, to support me. Oh, I knew I was being selfish, but I just wanted my Dad hale and hearty. How could I have thought of going to live in Italy when I knew my parents were going to need me to be home for them? They brought me up and now I owed it to them to be beside them when they needed help.

What stupid thought led me to believe that I could go away and leave them?

Dad's was big man, tall and well built. Actually, running to a bit of fat. He liked a beer and had never stinted on butter and sweets. Once home from work, he would sit and watch the television all evening. Not the healthiest of lifestyles. But for his heart to crack up like that and break down. No-one expected that to happen.

Pieta, watching the look of shocked fear on my face, immediately got on the phone to the airport to find us the earliest flight. I packed a few essentials and we went straight to the airport.

'What did your Mother say?' Pieta asked me as I sat in quiet misery on the plane.

'Just that he had had a heart attack and they are treating him. She says he is having an Angiogram to see what damage has been done.'

'I know it's very easy for me to say it, but he's in good hands and I'm sure he will be alright.'

I took his hand; I needed some comfort at that moment. I was glad he was there with me, but I just wanted my

Dad.

We had to fly into Gatwick, not Stanstead. But it was the first flight we could get. Pieta went to hire a car, so we could drive to the hospital. It was a quiet journey, I couldn't speak, but there were terrible thoughts going around my head. I felt selfish and thought it was a lesson to be learned. I should think of other people and not just me. I'd been so focused on my own happiness that I have not given much thought to the other people around me. I couldn't leave them now, could I? Go abroad and leave my parents. They have no other children and they'd need me to look after them in time. As they got older, if Dad did. What if he died? Oh, God I can't lose him. Just when everything was coming together.

We finally got to the hospital and found out which ward to go to. Dad was sitting up in bed, which was a surprise. He had no tubes coming out of him. He was cheerful.

'I've had the angiogram and I need a little bit of Angioplasty, which they are going to do possibly tomorrow. Be a couple of days then before I can go home. I should be able to go on Saturday.'

'What's one of them? An Angioplasty?' I asked.

'Oh, it's amazing, they put a deflated balloon up the artery from my leg, and then inflate it where the blockage is. Be right as rain after that. The doctor says I can be awake and watch it on the big screen. How fantastic is that?'

'Apart from the diet you have to go on and you have to give up smoking. And start doing some serious exercise. Proper stuff, not just wandering around the golf course until you get to the nineteenth hole,' Sheila said, leafing through some information books they had been given. She looked far more relaxed than I expected. I couldn't understand why neither of them were worried. It's a big thing, a heart attack.

'I thought you were dying. I thought I was going to lose you. I was so scared.'

'Oh goodness Fran, When I phoned your Mum, I thought I had made it plain that this was not a major heart attack. Your Dad is going to be fine. If he keeps to the instructions,' she said with a pointed glare at Dad.

'Just a gentle reminder to tell me to start looking after myself.'

'Gentle? A heart attack?'

Pieta came to me and put his arm round my shoulders. I leaned into him. Grateful that I had him to rely on in a time of crisis. He proved himself and was only concerned for me.

'I'm sorry to have spoiled your holiday. How is it all going anyway?' Dad asked

'My family love her, just as I do.' Pieta told him. I've not seen much of her. My sisters claimed her immediately and whisked her off shopping.'

'Happy days then,' Sheila said picking up another off the pile of leaflets.

'So, when I'm well enough to travel I can come over and see you?'

'I've not moved yet, Dad,' I said rather too emphatically, at which I felt Pieta stiffen his hold.

I went to see Dad every day in the hospital and when he came home. The first time I arrived at the house I was shocked to see him digging out a vegetable bed.

'Should you be doing that?'

'Doctors' orders, nothing too straining but this is light work and I have to keep moving.'

'Really? Doesn't look like light work to me, that

ground is rock hard. How long since you grew any vegetables in that patch?'

'I concede, it's been a few years, but I'm enjoying it, getting the old muscles working. Yep, more exercise and less of most of everything else. It was only a warning shot apparently and no lasting damage was done. I now have to make it stronger, my heart that is. If I'm not to be an invalid. I can lead a perfectly normal life. When you move out abroad, I'll be fit enough to come out and see you sooner than we'd hoped.'

'I'm not so sure I'm going yet.'

'What? Why ever not? Pieta isn't moving over here is he?'

'No, he can't possibly do that.'

'So why the big change of mind. Because of me? My dear I'll be a fitter man than I ever was and healthier. I'm thinking of getting another dog, to make me walk more. It's three years since we lost Boris, I do miss having a dog in the house. It'll get me out more, plenty of exercise, just what the doctor ordered. You mustn't put your life on hold for us.'

'How can I leave you, both of you?'

'You can because that's what children do. They go off and live their own lives and make their parents proud. Your Mum and I are sorted. You have all your life to live. Don't make us regret it. We, neither of us, want to hold you back.'

'I don't know, Dad. How can I possibly be happy about going? What if the next time it is a bad one? I don't feel right about leaving you.'

I wondered how I thought I deserved all this happiness. What's so very special about me that I could have my life just the way I wanted it? There's always something we have to give back for all the good things.

Perhaps I should just be happy that I have my children and stay and look after my parents. Let Pieta go? Let him live an unencumbered life? Would I always be worried sick about the parents if I was away in Italy? Oh, I know it is only a two- and half-hour flight, but I'd not be here, would I? How am I going to do this?

'My dear girl, if I do as the doctors tell me I will not be having another one. I'm already fitter now than I was before the attack. You mustn't think that we can't look after ourselves. We're not your responsibility. Your Mum and I are perfectly able to look after ourselves. I have Sheila and she now has Michael. You have to go and live your own life. You have at last found where in life you're supposed to be, and you must follow that.'

'Oh Dad, can I really do that. Be happy being away from you?'

'Of course, you can, and we'll be able to pop out to you any time. Next time you see me I'll be two stone lighter and only drinking red wine, and unfortunately much less of it. Go, go to be with your man. Let him help you bring up my grandchildren. I can retire soon, and we can pop over to see you lots and lots.'

I began to see how much I had overreacted at Dad being ill. But the words Heart Attack had made my blood run cold and I really was frightened at the thought of losing them. I'm a great believer in Karma and thought because I had the utter cheek to be happy that it was coming after me to bite me on the bum. I was still unsure if I wanted to lose the time, I had left with them by being away from them. But I loved Pieta so much and already regretted the years I've not been able to be with him. We've a lot of time to recapture and make good.

Dad and I went indoors for a cup of tea, Ginger tea for

both of us. He said he had found it and liked it and didn't need sugar in it like his normal tea. It was very nice, and I found myself wondering if it was available in the Italian supermarkets. I expect it is, if not I'll get Dad to send me some over. If I go.

After I left Dad, I needed some thinking time so drove to the local park. The one where I used to play as a child. Plonking myself down on a bench near the playground I went over the pros and cons of leaving to be with my man in Italy.

I'd been so focused on what I wanted it didn't occur to me that my parents would actually want me to go and live the life I was always meant to live. That maybe they would be happier knowing I was settled. As Dad said they would worry more to see me struggle to bring up two children alone. He made me see that going and being with Pieta would make them happier than staying behind. I felt a huge weight lift and the panic I'd felt fading along with the worry easing, also made me see that he was right. I had to go live my own life and trust that we had plenty more years to enjoy.

Feeling so much happier about going and knowing I was leaving both my parents in the good hands of Sheila and Michael I went home to Pieta.

He'd been out to visit George and when I got home, he asked how Dad was. I told him what we'd discussed about Dad's health. Not my worry about leaving the parents though. But he must have had an inkling because when I mentioned sorting a moving date to Italy, his face glowed with happiness.

Pieta

I had been taking Fran to see her Dad but made an

excuse to go and see George one day. I thought she needed to talk to him by herself and settle her mind. I knew she was having second thoughts about moving to Italy and was frightened that her parents couldn't cope without her here at home. I could understand that, although there are three of us, I really missed Mamma when she was here In England. Although she's spending much more time in Italy now, I'd noticed. I was trying to work out how we could get to see each other if Fran decided to continue to live here and I had to go home. I can leave work much more now as I have excellent staff and so wouldn't need to be at either the farm or the hotel all the time. But it would put a great strain on our relationship to be apart so much.

Now that I'd found her, I was not letting my Fran go again. It would work but only after a fashion. And I'd not get to see my children as much as I'd like either. Maybe I could sell everything in Italy and move to England. If Fran really wanted to stay close to her parents that would be an option. Not one I'd relish but I'll never be apart from her again.

I'd spent too many years waiting for this love. One of us had to make a big move. Either Fran or me. Up till this time it had been expected that Fran would make this sacrifice but why should it not be me? I had been thinking this all the time I was being shown round George's distribution centre. By the time I arrived back at Fran's house I'd almost made up my mind that I would make my home here in England.
If I had to, to keep Fran.

After seeing her father, I could see a glow of happiness that was comfortable about Fran. She had finally put all her fears at rest and was content with her decision. She was coming with me. I was so happy, and I knew I'd let it show that I'd been worried about it all. We talked long into the night about her fears, about mine and at last we reached an understanding and a stage in our love that we could hold onto for ever after.

Fran

After our long talk well into the night, we decided that the doctors would be our next visit to ascertain when would be best for me to make the journey.

'I wouldn't leave it much after the six-month mark, as you are expecting twins. They do tend to come a bit earlier than single babies. So, for a big move like that sometime around March at the latest. I can get all your paperwork together for the Italian doctors and they may want you to book a time for either a caesarean section or a day to be induced. But sometimes the babies decide just when they are coming into the world,' The doctor told us.

So, we were looking at March, then I would be able to move to Italy to be with my lovely man. We discussed it with Charley and Sam who were made up about it. Sam was really looking forward to having the house and had decided on a nursery for Dylan.

Mum said she would give me a month to settle in before she came with Michael to see us, she was already looking at brochures when Pieta said they would be able to stay at the farm. Dad and Sheila said they would come in May. But then they decided to swap those dates over between them for Mum to come in May and Dad before, in April. As Mum said I'd be nearing eight months by then and all being well our bambini may make an appearance around that time. She may even stay on to see them, as a retired lady she didn't only have to have a two-week holiday. I'm not too sure about a prolonged stay. And how'd she get on with Mamma, for such a long time. They did still spark off each other. Both elegant ladies, Mamma with her black hair and Mum with hers pure white. But trim of figure and much the same height. Perhaps they'd better go shopping together, just to make sure they don't buy the same outfit for our wedding.

Having finally made my decision I was at last content. The over the moon happiness was still there, but I was more settled in my mind. I realised I had been expecting it to all go wrong. But Pieta had proved to be as caring and loving whatever I had decided to do. And he wasn't going anywhere. After our long talk we set about planning our flights and packing the belongings that I would want to take. Pieta helped me to pack up the studio. I sent my letter out to my clients telling them I was taking maternity leave. I also appraised them of the new location of the company. I said I would let them know when I was ready to start taking commissions again. There were a few bits of furniture that had belonged to my Grandma that I wanted to take with me. We arranged for them to be sent in a container to Italy, to my new home along with my artist easel and more bits from the studio.

This was really going to happen. I was going to be with the man I have loved since I was eighteen years old.

Just him, me and our bambini. Oh, and the rest of his family.

Printed in Poland
by Amazon Fulfillment
Poland Sp. z o.o., Wrocław